Dropping Out

a tree-change novel-in-stories

Danielle de Valera

OLD TIGER BOOKS

OLD TIGER BOOKS
Dropping Out: a tree change novel-in-stories
Danielle de Valera

Cover design by James T Egan, Bookfly Design
Cover photograph of the Smiths' house, Upper Main Arm, NSW by David Liddle, Heritage Photographs, Balmain, Sydney.

ISBN-13: 978-0-9942545-2-6
ISBN-10: 0-9942545-2-1

Set in Minion Pro and Vidaloka

Published in the United States by Old Tiger Books

For Matthew Lambourne, who showed me the Northern Rivers of New South Wales.

Praise for Dropping Out:

No other writer in Australia captures so perfectly the spirit of a place.

Susan Geason, author: the cult Syd Fish novels

This entertaining set of stories is a penetrating evocation of the alternative culture of the 1980s. Roaming through detailed lives of the Northern Rivers of New South Wales, it is a convincingly nostalgic recollection, possibly from the inside.

Peter Baldwin, author: *Curragundi Tales*

Each thread of this collection is skilfully woven into an emotive tapestry that depicts the lives, loves and fates of some of the North Coast dropouts of the 1970s and 1980s, then broadens to conjure for the reader an unusual and ethereal vision of the future.

Shaune Lafferty Webb, author: *Bus Stop on a Strange Loop, Cold Faith*

There's a sense of wonder about these unique, and sometimes whimsical stories. For this American reader, it's the feeling of being a visitor to an unfamiliar universe which manages to border and overlap the more familiar one with the humanity of its characters. Disturbingly delightful.

C S McClellan, author: *Privileged Lives and Other Lies*

De Valera's prose is fresh and surprising ... the stories are all slice-of-life pieces, but they're far from predictable ... It makes for a great beach read, whether on the coast of New South Wales or the other side of the world.

Kirkus Reviews

Short story readers looking for an interconnected set of Australian lives and experiences on the fringes of society and life will find much to relish in *Dropping Out*. It is highly recommended ...

Diane Donovan, Senior Reviewer, *Midwest Book Review*

Contents

Preface

Following the Aquarius Festival in Nimbin in 1973, many people came to the Northern Rivers. For the most part, they were young. Full of hopes and dreams. Arriving with few resources, they rented disused banana-packing sheds, abandoned dairies and empty farmhouses for peppercorn rents. Most of them didn't have much money; some were on the dole. Nevertheless, these young people and their subsequent families injected much-needed cash into the area at a time when many of the little towns were dying, empty shop fronts beginning to appear in their main streets. Brunswick Heads still had its fishing fleet and coop, but the bottom had fallen out of the dairy industry, the whaling station at Byron Bay had closed and the meatworks at Belongil was struggling to survive. The area was in the hiatus between primary production and what would eventually become its lifeblood—tourism. Finding very few jobs available, the newcomers created cottage industries, and arts and crafts.

That was the upside. The downside was the toll the country took on people who were unused to it, people with insufficient financial resources and little or no family support. Some made it. Others, miles from anywhere, sometimes on foot, went down to alcohol, drugs, psychosis and loneliness—Australian poet Henry Lawson knew what he was talking about when he wrote in the late 1890s about "the maddening sameness of the … trees".

The stories in this collection were written over a period of twenty-five years. In them, I hoped to convey the sense of a particular time now gone, and to depict just a few of the characters who adorned the Far North Coast in the 1980s and onwards, and the fates that befell them. There were so many wonderful characters. I couldn't portray them all. In this book, I hope I have managed to recreate just a few of them.

D de V

Acknowledgments

This book owes its existence to many people.

I'd like to thank my beta readers: Shaune Lafferty Webb, Tony Moore, Carolyn David, Paul Smith, Denise Burton, Tara Sariban, Andrew Scobie, Peter Baldwin, C S McClellan and Beverly Lang.

A special mention must go to help I received far beyond the call of duty from Paul Smith with graphics, and US author C S McClellan for her invaluable advice on covers.

Bernard Delaney gave me wonderful insider advice on "Busting God", and Matthew Lambourne provided meticulous information on the Brunswick River and all things tidal.

My children Sasha Sariban and Tara Sariban, and Sasha's wife Babs Wheeler continued their unfailing support.

There were, as is usual for this area, local characters too numerous to mention.

My thanks to you all.

D de V

Dropping Out

a tree-change novel-in-stories

Danielle de Valera

OLD TIGER BOOKS

1
Busting God

1986

I loved the work too well. That was the problem. Even sitting in my kitchen nursing two cracked ribs, the contents of the house trashed around me, I still loved it.

But I was growing older.

I watched what I ate. I sweated at karate and ran miles every day so that I could stay in the field.

Still, I grew older.

Reg Mulcahey was leaning against my kitchen sink, looking worried. He pulled a packet of Camels from his pocket, lit two and passed one to me.

"Why didn't you tell those cops you were a narc? Christ, Michael!"

I wrenched a packet of frozen peas from the freezer and

sat down with the packet held against my rapidly closing eyelid.

"What'd you expect me to do, Reg—blow a cover I've been working on for months?"

"Well, y' cover's blown now," Reg drawled. "I had to show them my ID to get them off you; they can send someone else into that nightclub. By the way, The Eagle wants to see you. That's why I came."

The CEO had eyes that seemed to see right through you. That's why we called her The Eagle. That afternoon she was in a hurry. She was due at a high-powered press conference on narcotics at two. She could barely make the time to tell me I was taking a paid trip to the Northern Rivers to bust a heroin dealer everyone up there called God. She threw my new ID papers at me and told me to catch the next train out of Sydney.

"Where exactly would you like me to go, ma'am?"

"If you're meaning a town, O'Neill—try Murwillumbah."

My clothes were torn and bloodied. I was still holding the packet of peas to my eye. She didn't seem to notice.

"I'd like to take Azure with me," I ventured.

"Nix to that, you're taking Johnson with you. Not on the same train, of course."

I knew Baby Johnson from Vietnam. Everything he touched turned to trouble. I didn't want to go anywhere with Baby, but it was no use arguing.

The peas had melted. I pitched them into her wastepaper basket and turned to go.

"O'Neill?" She got me just as I reached the doorway, a trick of hers. "When you come back—you do intend to come back, don't you?—I expect you to take that desk job.

Why don't you marry that girl and settle down?" she hurled after me. "You're too old for field work anyway."

We had a bad scene at Central Station when Azure discovered we were going north for some time. I'd told her we were going to visit my mother in Wollongong.

"What about my elephant collection?" she cried.

I bundled her on to the train. "I'll get you another."

Maybe I should've felt guilty but, as Mahitabel the cat said to Archie the cockroach, wot-the-hell. There were bound to be plenty of elephants in northern New South Wales.

Elephants you can always get.

Murwillumbah didn't seem to be the place to find God. The trail led south to Ballina. We rented a small fibro cottage on the dunes in a hamlet called New Brighton, a safe forty ks or so from Ballina. Then I linked up with Baby, who'd scored a disused banana-packing shed in the mountains outside Mullumbimby, and together we worked at slotting into the low life in what the sign on the highway declared was THE BIGGEST LITTLE TOWN IN AUSTRALIA.

I went home every night to New Brighton when I could, and sat with Azure on the verandah overlooking the empty, windswept beach. At dusk the Cape Byron lighthouse would begin to flash every thirteen seconds. If the tide was high, the prawn fleet would be heading out to sea, emerging from the Brunswick River three ks to the south of us. One by one, the trawlers would go out over the treacherous bar, a space of about four hundred metres between them. At night we could see their deck lights strung out like Chinese lanterns along the horizon.

They say the rock walls at the river's entrance were built back in the '50s to give the fishing fleet safe access to the sea. Whatever. They were certainly there when my father brought us here for a holiday in 1960. We couldn't afford to rent a house, so we pitched a big tent behind the dunes, bushranger-style, and cooked over an open fire. In those days there were very few rangers, and they didn't have the gung-ho attitude they have today.

The heat, the stillness, the quality of the light in summer gave a strange timeless feeling to the back to the dunes, like stepping into another dimension. The whole time we were there I wandered the beach like someone in a dream. It used to piss my father off. He wanted me to join the rest of the family in digging for pippis, but I had no time for that; I was hatching a plan. I wasn't going to be stuck in some dead-end job for the rest of my life, like he was. I wasn't going to be poor forever.

Like they say, the best-laid plans of mice and men . . .

There was only one downside to New Brighton. Spiders. Every night they spun their webs from banksia tree to banksia tree across the narrow path to the beach. Every morning there they'd be, swinging head-high in the centres of their three-metre webs. I smashed and banged at them each a.m. while Azure cowered behind me in tears. They were only Golden Orb spiders, handsome fellows with black-and-gold stripy legs, but she had a phobia about spiders.

If I forgot to do this before I left, Azure would stand in

the backyard and wail for Star.

"Star, *Staar!* Please help me!" And Star would come over from her house and gently remove all the spiders with a broom.

Star seemed a bona fide hippie, though Azure assured me she'd once had a high-flying job in Sydney. Separated from her husband because of his violence, she lived with her two pre-school boys in the next house on the dunes with a vegetable garden, compost heap, bicycle, pension—the lot. I thought her naive. The first day she met me, she showed me the dope plant she was growing to buy a pot-bellied stove for the winter.

"It gets cold here when the southerlys blow, Michael," she said, long dark hair hanging down over her Indian print dress, tanned, tow-haired toddler on one hip. "There are cracks in the floorboards and Ptolemy's asthmatic."

That wood stove was her Holy Grail, God was mine, and we both thought like Jesuits. Countless times in the night I saved The Plant from being ripped off by threatening total strangers with violence. Towards the end I started to complain.

"Azure, tell Star to harvest that bloody plant. There's a wood stove's worth there now. What kind of a name's Star, anyhow?"

"Her real name's Stella, but she doesn't like it."

"Hmph. Tell her to cut that plant."

Azure would've been very lonely that autumn without Star and the two littlies. I was away a lot.

God was proving difficult to find.

I was looking for someone called David, who was said by one informant to have connections. It wasn't that he sold foils out of his socks in the upwardly-mobile Top Pub but simply that he'd been here since the Nimbin Festival. He knew everybody.

I hoped that if we hung with David long enough he'd lead us to God, or at least to one of God's connections, but patience was never my strong suit. In the end, I came to the point directly.

"Do you know how to find God?" I asked him one night, when Baby and I were hanging out in his shack eight ks from the Mullumbimby post office.

He'd been sitting on the bed, smoking and listening to Muddy Waters on his CD player. Now he leapt to his feet, scattering ashtrays and empty stubbies, and got me in a headlock from behind. He was strong and fast for a bloke on the disability pension.

"*What are you?*" he shouted.

I thought, Christ, are we sprung?

Baby didn't even look up from the Conan novel he was reading on an upturned packing case.

Dave was still shouting. "Are you some kind of fuckin' born-again Christian? If you are, get the fuck out of here!"

Dave cherished a theory that a local Christian cult called the True Vine had destroyed his marriage by converting his wife Doreen, who had been a first-class alkie, and who was now one of the top cats in the True Vine industry. Doreen claimed she still loved Dave. She kept sending people around to convert him.

I squawked that I wasn't a Christian, and he released me.

"You don't use, do you?"

"I just want to deal a bit, make some money. Azure and I want to get married."

This answer seemed to pacify him. "Can you get into town Wednesdays? Say round one at the Bottom Pub."

He threw two single mattresses on to the kitchen floor and blew out the kerosene lamp. Baby and I lay down in the clothes we stood up in. Possums clattered over the old tin roof. The bull koalas called weirdly like cattle. And for once I didn't have any bad dreams.

When I woke up in the morning, Baby was gone, and a local freak called The Captain was leaning against the door frame, smoking a rollie. He was wearing a white dress with lace trimming.

I shouldn't have been that hungover, though we did get into the rum at the end, so I looked away. But when I looked back, he was still standing there.

"I suppose you're wondering why I'm wearing this dress," he said.

"Not especially." I went out to have a piss, then I came back inside and made myself a cup of coffee.

"I lost my clothes," The Captain explained.

"Uh huh."

"Well, I didn't lose them really; I just mislaid them."

"Uh huh." I stirred the sugar into my coffee and studied him.

He was around thirty, about ninety kilos, a hundred and eighty-three centimetres—and fit. Very fit for a freak. Why they called him The Captain was a mystery.

"When I wanted to leave I couldn't find my clothes

anywhere," he continued, "so I went through the chick's wardrobe. Well, I couldn't go home starkers, now could I?"

"You've got great taste, Captain," I said. "It looks good on you."

He flashed me a grin from under his mop of naturally blond hair streaked pink and green and purple with food colouring.

"Good," he said. "As soon as the shops open I'm going to walk into town and have breakfast at The Country Kitchen."

"You do that, Captain," I said.

I decided to raid his dilly bag as soon as I got the chance and have his ID checked out by the bureau.

The Bottom Pub specialised in rednecks and footballers. Even at one o'clock on a Wednesday, the bar was crowded. I took my drink into the beer garden, ordered the compulsory counter lunch and waited for the connection to show.

He joined me almost immediately, wearing the standard summer apparel affected by the middle-class men of the town—long socks, long shorts and a shirt with barber's pole stripes. The gut hung over the belt. For an instant I wondered if he was an off-duty cop, but he didn't have any of the mannerisms.

He introduced himself as Wayne. "David tells me you're interested in God."

In all my years in this business, I've never met a go-between I could take to. I never liked their style; they had no class.

"Let's just say," I muttered, "I hope my prayers will be answered. Does God really deliver?"

Two lunches landed heavily on the table in front of us: T-bones with French fries, some ornamental lettuce and tomato, and a sprig of triple-curl parsley.

The waitress took one look at me and went to fetch the publican.

"You wanted four weights, is that right?" Wayne asked. "You got the bread?"

Bread was Wayne's best shot at street cred. Like I said, no style. I ratted around in my calico dilly bag and produced ten thousand dollars. Wayne didn't seem to mind the dubious state of the bills and smiled as he counted them.

"Yes, I think we should be able to do business."

I picked up a chip. Out of the corner of my eye, I could see the publican bearing down on our table at Mach 3.

"O'Brien?" The publican's voice boomed out across the beer garden. "Is that you, O'Brien?" He was short-sighted.

Wayne waved a well-cared-for hand. "It's okay, Tom, he's with me. Honey," he said to the waitress mopping our table with a grubby cloth, "get us two more beers, will you?" He pushed a ten-dollar bill into her ample cleavage. "Thanks a lot, love, keep the change."

The publican disappeared. The greenery swallowed him up. The waitress returned like magic and smashed the beers down in front of us.

Wayne watched her retreating form. "Where were we? Oh yes, I guess you'll be wanting to see the goods."

He took out what looked like a packet of Drum and placed it on the table between us. Inside was a plastic sandwich bag containing approximately four ounces of what appeared to be heroin.

I stared at the packet sitting there between the red plastic salt and pepper shakers. There were other people in the beer garden: a couple of families with small children, and four girls I recognised from the Commonwealth Bank.

"You want to test it?" Using the end of his fork, Wayne shovelled enough for one hit on to the torn-off corner of his paper serviette. "Here, make yourself comfortable."

I took the stuff, locked myself in the toilet and tested it with the little kit I carried. It was the real thing. I waited long enough to have shot it and returned to the table.

Wayne smiled at me. "Good gear eh?"

I tried to appear mellow. "Look," I said, it was now or never. "I'm in a position to make a much bigger deal than this. Much bigger . . ." I let him hang for a while. "Can I trust you? I work for someone. And the person I work for has got unlimited finance."

"Unlimited finance?" The magic words. "How much are we talking?"

I paused. "Two hundred thousand—maybe more. Can you supply that much?"

Wayne nodded. "Can you get all that bread together in one place?"

"No worries," I lied. "The man I work for is big in Sydney. But . . ." I pretended to drift a bit, "an amount of money like that . . . you understand. I'd have to hand it to The Man myself."

Wayne shook his head. "God never gives interviews."

I took a stab. "Not even for a quarter of a million?"

Wayne considered for a while, then he picked up the Drum packet and went away to make a phone call from the telephone on the bar.

I expected a blank No to my proposal; it sounded too

much like a set-up to me, but Wayne returned as I was finishing my steak and said, "He's going to consider it. Give me your ID."

I gave him my fake pension card, in which I was called O'Brien, the name I was using up here. Wayne took down the relevant details. No doubt favours would be exchanged, and I'd be punched through somebody's data base. He was about to return the card when my address registered in his lizard brain. So I lived next door to his no-good wife Stella. Was she keeping her nose clean?

He'd been married to Star? I couldn't believe it. I wasn't going to tell this slime ball how well she and Baby were getting along. He'd probably have Baby beaten to within an inch of his life. Or worse. I feigned nodding off.

Wayne pushed the ID and the Drum packet across the table to me. "You'd better get going now. You're ruining the tone of Tom's establishment. We'll be in touch by the end of the week."

"How will you know where to find me?"

Wayne smiled. "God'll find you. God is everywhere. He's omniscient."

"I think you mean omnipresent." I slung the price of the second beer down on to the table, picked up the gear and walked out.

"By the way, your friend's in gaol!" Wayne called after me. "Drunk and disorderly."

It was the last day of autumn. We lay on the lawn on the headland opposite the Beach Hotel in Byron Bay. Azure and I were half under a hibiscus bush with double pink flowers.

The Captain, who'd been sticking to us like glue, lay beside us with his latest girlfriend Julie. She was a wisp of a thing with scrappy black hair and a see-through Indian arrangement.

She was also a dedicated junkie. I wondered if Captain knew that.

I was waiting for word from God. It was Saturday now, and I was still waiting. I was drifting away on the sound of the sea when Captain jabbed me in the ribs.

A person of indeterminate sex in long white robes and with equally flowing grey hair was approaching across the grass. S/he stopped in front of The Captain and Julie.

"I am the current manifestation of the Archangel Gabriel!"

"Yeah yeah."

"The only redemption is Jesus."

"Piss off!"

"Hear me, man, for I am the one sent to show thee the way to God."

I sprang to my feet and dragged the angel behind the hibiscus bush.

"Ballina," the voice said, dropping an octave in three seconds. He pressed a piece of paper into my hand. A car had driven up. It stood at the kerb with its engine running. The angel raced to it in a flurry of robes and jumped in, flashing purple socks. As the car drove off I unfolded the note. It read:

Paradise Motel. 2 p.m. Sunday. Divine Worship.

"What a funny place for a church service," Captain said,

reading over my shoulder.

I went back to the Mullumbimby police station and bailed Baby out. I had a feeling I was going to need him.

Baby and I checked into the Paradise Motel at noon on Sunday. We'd barely got into the room when the phone rang and a heavy voice I didn't recognise told me to "Get rid of that gorilla".

"I think they mean you, Baby Chops."

"Well, I ain't going." Baby was sprawled on one of the twin beds, guzzling designer beer from the bar fridge and checking over the gun he'd been carrying under his outsize flannelette shirt. The ubiquitous Conan novel lay by his side.

I walked along the corridor and knocked on the door of the room next to ours. Inside, Reg and the surveillance team had everything organised: holes had been drilled through the wall adjoining ours, cameras and microphones had been set up.

"I hope you know what you're doing, O'Neill," Reg said darkly when he saw me. "You don't think this guy's going to front up without heavies, and they're sure to be carrying."

I started back to my room before Reg could ruin my nice adrenalin rush.

"I know you're crazy, O'Neill," he hissed down the corridor after me. "But whatever you do, don't leave the motel. Don't leave Mother!"

Half an hour later, the phone rang again. This time it was Wayne.

"I thought that bloke was in jail. Why is he here?"

I began to feel uneasy. Maybe God was omniscient, after all. Did he know about the agents who were all over the building? Maybe he intended to roll me for the money and string my body up from the clock tower of the Biggest Little Town in Australia as a warning to any other narcotics agent who might think of disturbing his lucrative empire.

On the bed lay the suitcase containing twenty thousand dollars, all I had been given by the department to show. Underneath the top layers, the rest was cut-up paper. A fact that made me nervous.

At precisely two p.m. there was a knock on our door. It wasn't God, however, who came in. It was Wayne.

"Did you get all the bread?" he asked.

I indicated the suitcase lying open on the bed beside Baby. Wayne advanced on it as if to count the money.

I blocked his path. "Where's the gear? And where's God?"

Wayne gave me one of *those* smiles. "God's changed his mind. He wants me to do the deal for him." He produced two weights and threw them on to the bed. "That's the sample."

"Where's the rest?" I demanded as Baby tested the sample and counted out the money in marked one-hundred-dollar bills.

Wayne pocketed the notes. "The rest's at a safe house across town. You come with me. We can finish the deal there."

I got myself a beer from the bar fridge. I made a point of not offering him one, and in this small non-verbal way I conveyed my disapproval of his plan. Wayne then suggested we split the gear and the money into five separate lots. He'd bring each lot to the motel and we'd do the whole thing here.

It was no way to find God.

"Listen," I said to Wayne, "I'll level with you. My boss is Italian; I'm his right-hand man. *That* there," I pointed at Baby, "is his cousin. Look," I shoved the phone at him, "I've got to hand the money directly to God, they're my orders. And he's got to come too. You can't insult the boss's cousin."

Wayne hesitated. He flung a glance at Baby, who lay on the bed trying to look smouldering and Italian. Then he took the phone from my hand and started pressing numbers.

I wanted him to stay on the phone long enough for the call to be traced, so I went over to the window and pretended to study the landscape. Down below, a blonde with magnificent hair teetered out of the motel carrying a large shoulder bag. She wore a tight leather skirt, a leopard-print top and spike heels.

"Okay," Wayne said; he hadn't been on the phone long enough for a trace. "God says he understands. It's a lot of money. He'll be there."

"OK." I locked the briefcase and pocketed the keys. "Let's go."

We were flying on a wing and a prayer. With a suitcase full of paper money and two guns between us, we were driving away from all the security we'd had.

I was still optimistic. There'd been enough time for Reg to organise a tail for us, and Wayne was going to lead us to

God. All we had to do when we got there was stall for five minutes and the place would be surrounded by bureau agents. Wayne had patted us down in the hotel's parking lot and taken our unmarked Smith & Wessons, but he'd missed the Semmerling LM4 each of us carried in an ankle holster. Our possession of these five-shot pistols—small as a derringer but with much more stopping power—was unknown to the bureau, although we did have licences for them.

Out on the highway Wayne started glancing in the rear-view mirror a lot. "Did you put a tail on us, O'Brien? Those bitches are following us."

Three cars behind, two young women, their hair whipping in the wind, were zooming along in a white sports car.

"Maybe they like our looks," I offered. "Drive slower."

"I want the redhead," Baby rumbled from the back seat.

Wayne drove faster. He executed a hard left turn and some very fancy rights, and we found ourselves at the Richmond River. The vehicular ferry was on our side. There were no bridges.

Wayne drove the Volvo on to the old ferry. He slipped the ferryman fifty dollars. The ferryman slipped the tail chain in place and started up the engine. The young women were left jumping up and down on the river bank.

I lit a cigarette and thought as the ferry pulled out into the broad river. Unlike Cliff Richard, we weren't wired for sound. Now we were completely on our own.

"Baby," I said, as we bumped off the ferry on the other side of the river, "have you rung your mother lately?"

"My mother's been dead for six years," Baby snarled.

I twisted around and looked him hard in the eye. "I think

you should ring her real soon," I hissed. "I'm sure she'd like to know where you are."

Wayne had pulled off the highway and was speeding east along a sandy track. He drove into an old garage opposite a small cottage near the beach. It was a very isolated spot.

"You go in first," I told Wayne. "I'm not going in with all this money until I know for certain God's there with the gear."

Wayne strode in. Soon a person fitting God's surveillance photos appeared at the front window. Wayne stood in the doorway of the cottage, holding up a clear plastic bag full of something white. As we watched he opened it up, dipped his finger into it, put down the bag where we could still see it and walked back to the car.

"Taste it," he said venomously, holding out his finger to me.

I had no intention of tasting it. Instead I scraped enough of the powder off his finger and tested it with the kit I'd carried with me. It was real all right.

"Okay, Wayne," I said, "blame it on my toilet training, but I'm not a trusting man. I'm going to leave Baby here. If anything happens to me, well, let's just say he knows who you are and where your family lives."

Baby produced the Semmerling from his ankle holster and waved it at Wayne from the back seat. It was then I noticed the seat was littered with miniature bottles of alcohol, all empty, which he must have stolen from the motel's bar fridge.

"Gimme the car keys," he slurred.

Wayne stepped back out of arm's reach. "You'll have to shoot me first. You're not driving off to get reinforcements and rip us off."

I would've loved to shoot him, but it wouldn't have looked good in a court of law. I got out of the car and walked into the house with Wayne. I hoped Baby was a good runner. The last phone box I'd seen was at the highway turn-off, three ks back.

Seated in the living room, Siamese cat on his knee, was an elegant man in his early sixties. He was holding a tumbler of Scotch and ice. He wore cream slacks, an Italian-knit sweater and a cream cravat. I imagined a yacht somewhere.

"O'Brien," Wayne said deferentially, though the deference was not for me, "may I introduce Mr Westmoreland." He dumped the plastic bag full of heroin down on the coffee table.

"Mind if I look around?"

God stirred. "If it'll make you feel more comfortable, Mr O'Brien, go ahead, go ahead."

I prowled through the house. When I reached the kitchen, I saw why he was so cool: two heavies with shoulder holsters were playing Black Jack at the kitchen table. They cut me hard glances as I passed down the hallway.

"Happy?" Westmoreland asked when I returned to the living room.

Anything but. I had entered God's lair without backup. Now what?

"How about a drink?" I hedged. "Scotch is fine. No water."

Wayne pressed another of the Swedish tumblers into my hand.

God held up his. "To us!"

We drank. I wondered if Baby had change for the phone.

"And now," God said, "the briefcase, Mr O'Brien. If you please."

It was no use trying to stall any longer. I placed the briefcase on the coffee table and tossed Wayne the keys. As he came forward I stepped back three paces and pulled the Semmerling out of my ankle holster.

Wayne opened the case and riffled past the top layer. Cut-up pieces of paper fluttered to the floor.

"Shit," he said and slumped into a chair.

"My name is O'Neill," I said as quietly as I could. "I'm a member of the Narcotics Bureau. This place is surrounded. Be very quiet please, and lie on the floor, face down."

Wayne complied but God remained where he was. "Do you mind if I sit, Mr O'Neill? This is something of a shock." He placed a hand on his chest. "My heart, you know."

Well, I wanted him alive, so I acquiesced. Long minutes went by. Where was Baby? From where I stood, I could see into the hallway that led to the kitchen. Wayne had buried his face in his hands. God was fiddling nervously with one arm of the chair.

I didn't hear the shots that came through the front window. The first bullet took me in the wrist, knocking the Semmerling from my hand. The second hit me in the shoulder, spinning me around. I knew then that the goons in the kitchen had somehow been alerted and that help *if* it came would not come soon enough for me.

The heavies came in. They kicked me a couple of times, just in passing. Suddenly I could see my own funeral: The Eagle looked resigned, Reg was boring someone, Azure was looking beautiful in black—and Baby was still searching for a phone.

I was passing out when in through the doorway leapt a leggy blonde in a tight skirt and leopard-print top. She was barefooted and carried a SWAT team semi-automatic which she waved about in an unfriendly fashion.

"*Freeze!*" she shouted. "Drop the guns—all of you!"

It was the young woman I'd seen coming out of the motel in Ballina.

"Honey," I said, "I don't know who you are, but you're in the right movie."

"Cut the crap, O'Neill." It was The Captain's voice. "Just pick up the guns."

After the bureau boys had come and gone, and their mobile doctor had patched me up ("You again, O'Neill?") I asked The Captain where he'd come from.

He smiled at me. He was still wearing the wig and the gear.

"The boot of the car," he answered. He was already into God's liquor cabinet. "I just climbed in and held it together with a bit of fencing wire. Want some of this? It's class stuff."

"Did Reg know about you?"

"Nah, I work alone. Like you used to, O'Neill. The Eagle sent me."

Baby had also turned his attention to the liquor cabinet. "What's this guy's real name, anyway?"

I helped myself to the Scotch. "Doyle," I answered. "Real name's Charles Doyle. But he calls himself Lawson these days. He'll probably go down for ten, get out in seven."

"What's gonna happen to the cat?' Baby indicated God's Siamese cat watching us balefully from the top of a bookcase.

"I'll give it to Azure; she likes cats. 'Specially Siamese."

"Sa-ay," Captain broke in, "are you going to take that desk job, O'Neill, make a little room for me? Ah'se just a po-ah country boay. Ah needs a break."

"Did anyone ever tell you you're a bastard, Captain?"

He doubled over. The long blonde wig bobbed fetchingly up and down as he laughed. I thought how he could make a fortune in Kings Cross.

"You can't stop, can you, O'Neill? You're just another fuckin' junkie. You're hooked!"

It was after ten when Baby arrived at the New Brighton house. We'd be gone by dawn, no sense in taking risks, but Azure and Star didn't know that. I decided I'd leave a note for Star. She could have anything we left in the house, and we'd be travelling light. If the painkillers the doctor had given me held out, I planned to carry Az to the car at the last moment. With luck, we'd be halfway to Sydney before she woke up and cracked on to what was happening.

The four of us lay back on beanbags, smoking God's dope, drinking God's Scotch and watching Ridley Scott's cut of *Blade Runner.* The air in the living room was thick with smoke. Even the cat was loaded.

At four in the morning, everyone was asleep but me. In the light from the guttering candles Azure's new collection of brass and crystal elephants accused me. I promised myself I'd chuck as many of them as I could into my kitbag when we were leaving.

I went outside. It was almost dawn. Already the spiders had finished spinning their webs across the path that led to the beach. I ripped out The Plant and pushed it in through one of Star's open windows, then I went and stood on the dunes.

A light wind was blowing, and the scent of the Caterpillar wattle mingled with the smell of the sea. What did I want with a desk job?

And yet . . .

There are times when I get tired of this existence and think that I'll get out while I still can. That's when I think I'd like a vegetable garden like Star's—even a compost heap, maybe. I'd like to plant some trees and stick around long enough to see them grow.

But then tomorrow comes and things seem different.

Yet I ask myself in the night when I can't sleep and the day has been particularly dangerous: how much longer do I think I can go on doing this?

Not much longer.

So will I take that desk job?

I don't know. I'm caught in a web of my own making, though caught isn't really the right word.

Like the spiders, I can stop any time I want to.

2

Star's Story

1979

She didn't look in the mirror as her hair fell around her, the hair her father had loved so much. She had gone into the salon on a whim; the place was empty. Perhaps the impulse to buzz-cut her hair was brought on by the anaesthetic.

"Have you got someone to take care of you when you get home?"

"Yes yes, I'll be fine."

Her face looked pale under the fluorescent lights. No make-up. Her eyes, caught in the salon's wall-sized mirrors, revealed too much. The hairdresser hacked at her long dark hair. Star looked down, studied other things. The hem of her designer power suit. Her sheer pantyhose. Her Italian high-heeled shoes.

They'd have to go. The whole effect had to go.

"There," the hairdresser said, shaking out the short

plastic cape she had fastened around Star's shoulders. Dabbing at the back of her neck with a soft brush.

Star bought a pair of Baxter's at a nearby shoe store. She bought a pair of jeans, a denim cap and two shirts at an op shop and changed her clothes in the cubicle, leaving the designer gear behind her. She bought a leather bomber jacket at a pawnshop in the next block—she was putting it on as she came out of the pawnbroker's and flagged down a taxi.

When the north bound Motorail pulled into Central Station, Star was the first person on it. She'd bought a ticket to the end of the line, Murwillumbah, but she figured she'd jump off wherever took her fancy.

The train slid out of the station. The whole mess was behind her.

After dinner the lights came on in the carriages. People settled down to their reading; some played cards. Star took the two sleeping pills the doctor had given her and slept, without dreaming, through the night. When she woke, late in the morning, the train was pulling into a small country town. Two bay horses stood in a paddock near the shunting yards.

As the train slowed the station sign slid by, black print on blue.

M U L L U M B I M B Y

She walked up the main street to the Top Pub, carrying nothing but a shoulder bag.

The horse came out, ran twice around the racetrack. The jockey on his back wore blue and black satin. The people in the grandstand cheered.

"Look, darling," Star's father said. His thick black hair shone in the sunlight; he looked like Robert Taylor in Ivanhoe. *"You'll be able to tell people when you're an old lady; you'll be able to say you saw 'Tulloch'."*

"Yes, Daddy," Star said. "But he wasn't racing."

Her father must've known then that he had a depressive on his hands, that the dark streak in her mother's family had found yet another home. But Star was the only child he had.

Every evening, before dinner, he sparred with her.

"Keep y' dukes up, girlie, always keep y' dukes up. They can't hit you if y've got y' dukes up."

He'd wanted a boy. Had planned to call him Jack.

Mullumbimby's Top Pub was just opening. People were straggling in. A man in his early thirties was hovering near the jukebox, wearing tailored shorts, long socks and a striped shirt. A business type, Star figured, looking for music to accompany a liquid lunch. He tried to catch her eye, but she ignored him.

Too straight.

Then she saw *him* from across the room. Tall, dark, saturnine. Drinking alone. There he sat, like a knight with a moat around him, and something about the image pulled her in.

His name was David. He was kind of fragile, an out-of-work schoolteacher whose wife ran *satori* workshops. He said she was his ex, but he'd called her his wife, Star noted. This usually meant trouble. He said the wife, the ex, whatever, made a killing on the new age circuits. Now she'd run off with someone he called The Great Outdoors.

On her way up the street Star had seen the woman who ran off with The Great Outdoors—hard to miss her with the Blue Heeler. When it was accidentally killed, David told Star over wines, his wife had skinned the carcase, tanned the hide. Now she was wearing the hide around town, tied about her shoulders like a tribal princess.

He called her Crystal. Star figured she was probably christened Doreen.

She got David drunk and asked him, point blank, moon on the moat's water lilies, if he wanted to get back with Crystal Doreen.

No, David said, this was *it;* no more mucking around, they were really finished this time.

Star decided to give the straight life one more try.

Her father was a diesel engineer, a clever man who'd educated himself out of the foundry by going to night school, a warrior who'd gone over the Kokoda Trail in '42 without a scratch.

He met Star's mother in Toowoomba in 1958. She was twenty-six and holding out for marriage. She came from a poor Black Irish family, the only one of twelve children who hadn't ended up working for the railway. She worked as a housemaid in the hotel Star's father frequented after foundry hours.

She didn't drink, spent all her money on clothes she de-

signed herself and had run up by a dressmaker. Jean Shrimpton had yet to scandalise Australia with the conservative mini-dress she wore to the Melbourne Cup in 1965. Star's mother's world was a world of fitted bodices, set-in sleeves, stockings and elasticised step-ins with suspenders.

She loved black. Even years later Star couldn't wear it.

When Star's father asked her mother to marry him, it must have seemed to her that working for one man couldn't be any harder than working in the pub.

David owned a German Shepherd called Harry. Which bit people. Harry would never bite you if he thought you were expecting it; he'd wait 'til you were off guard. It was too much for Star. She lived in town while David lived with Harry in an old timber cabin in the hills.

The cabin featured coloured glass windows from demolished houses, and no power. At night the scent of white ginger blossoms fought with the smell of wood smoke and kerosene.

One night they were drinking beer when David clouded over.

"I'm still in love with Crystal," he said.

The jazz from his battery-operated tape deck floated out into the night. Billie Holiday's "Strange Fruit" bought Star time to think. When David drank beer he regressed to Doreen. When he drank wine he swung Star's way.

She got rid of the beer. The consumption of wine rose to dizzying heights.

Another night David said, "I've always wanted to wear feathers in my hair—at the back, you know, like a brave. But

Crystal said it wasn't ethnically correct."

"Neither are business suits," Star said, "if you're not European."

So David started wearing feathers in his long black hair. He got *What Bird Is That?* out of the local library, and he started collecting feathers. He hadn't had a hobby before.

"Anything else you'd like to do?"

Candles guttered on the old pine table. Star could see the Big Dipper through the clear glass of the attic window.

"I want to paint. In oils. I started once but Crystal complained. She said—"

Star got in first. "Do it."

So David started painting. No one came up to her at parties to ask if he'd gone crazy.

She was five years old when she first heard her parents fighting in bed. After that she heard it often.

Her mother would be crying, "No! No!" Desperate, crazy. Her father would mutter something she couldn't hear. Then there would be sounds of a struggle. Her mother would shriek—but quietly. Then, very quickly, there would be no more struggle. Only the sound of her crying.

Afterwards she always said, "I wish I'd never married you."

As if that were some kind of defence.

In the morning everything would appear normal. Star's mother would be in the kitchen, wearing a floral dress, cooking bacon & eggs and fried bread, while the sun came through the embroidered curtains she had sewn by hand.

On Saturdays Star went with her father to the races. She was wild about horses. She kept asking for a pony every Christmas. It was a dream. They lived in a one-bedroom flat in an inner suburb of Brisbane, part of an old house that had been converted into flats during World War II.

The woman who owned the flats lived in the best of them with a clutter of dark Victorian furniture and two canaries. She had lost her fiancé in the war in the Pacific, over twenty-one years before. Other people's children were not her cup of tea.

Star hated her with the fierce there-is-only-black-and-white of childhood. She could still remember the woman's face as she hissed at her from the upstairs window:

"Don't pick those flowers!"

David had been asked by his landlady to vacate the shack; she'd found some reliable people who didn't have a dog. By now Harry had become the scourge of the shire, fording the creek and terrorising cattle on the other side. Farmers kept rolling up to the cabin in four-wheel drives, threatening to kill Harry if he touched another cow, but David just went on painting.

He had no money, had spent it all on paints. Against her better judgment, Star helped him to move into her place. They made various trips over a number of days. Eventually everything was gone but the double bed, his wedding gift from Doreen. They lashed the bed, with its legs in the air, to the roof-racks of Star's old Holden, and started down to the town.

It was half-past-three in the afternoon as they drove through the main street. As they approached the National Australia Bank she saw Doreen on the top step, folding fifty-dollar bills into her wallet.

A goods train had stopped on the level crossing ahead of them. Traffic had backed up for two hundred metres. They ground to a halt right outside the bank.

Doreen looked up from her money. She saw the bed.

Star couldn't remember fighting with Sebastian in the first six months of their marriage. If they did, they'd resolved it in bed.

At twenty she'd found herself thinking, almost against her will, of settling down. She chose Sebastian. He was a structural engineer, a clever man who made architects' designs stand up, become buildings. She seduced him with her hair, her long dark hair, which she used without compunction.

One night, eight or nine months into their marriage, they had an argument over dinner. He'd drunk too much. He hurled his plate at her.

She drove to the hospital, holding a towel over one eye, to get five stitches in the gash under her right eyebrow, while Sebastian remained at home. Brooding.

Next argument they had, he hit her. She hit him back—her father had taught her well—and the pattern was established. But he was much bigger and stronger than she.

She hung in there way past the use-by date. Days she couldn't disguise the marks she stayed at home, watching

Oprah on TV.

Sebastian swore, dark-eyed, that he would hunt her down and kill her if she left him. When she finally caught the train to Murwillumbah, she didn't tell even her closest friends, in case they inadvertently betrayed her.

Three weeks after David had moved into Star's rented house, they woke at dawn to the sound of pounding on the front door. Star went out to find Doreen on the top step, hissing like a boiler just before the explosion.

"Where's David?" she hissed.

"Not here."

His car was standing in the driveway.

"Allow me to enlighten you," Doreen said.

Star picked up an empty Chardonnay bottle that had rolled away into a corner of the enclosed verandah, and watched Doreen's eyes.

David had appeared behind Star in the hallway. He looked very pretty in the cotton sarong he always slept in. Two magpie feathers dangled from his hair.

"Just let me speak to her for a moment, Stella?"

Star went away and made herself a pot of tea; but she was the one who was stewing.

"What'd *she* want?" she asked when Doreen had driven away.

He was casual. "Oh, she just wanted to talk about the sale of the house—she wanted to know if it was all right with me."

"Oh yeah?" Star yelled. "Since when did Doreen ever care what anybody wants? It's against her principles."

Then they had a fight in which she brought up the dog.

"Do you know," she said, "that people say she ate that dog? She didn't just skin it—she *ate* it!"

"You don't understand!" David was screaming now, feathers bobbing. "She loved that dog! It was the only way she could feel it was still *part* of her. But you don't understand esoteric things like that!"

Star understood better than he imagined.

Dr Richardson was a wealthy man. The waiting room. The Russian ikons on the wall behind his antique desk. The elegant gardens in front of the beautifully restored terrace house from where he conducted his clinic.

The waiting room was full of women. As diverse as they were in looks and status, they had one thing in common: none of them could keep these children they felt growing inside them, so much a part of them despite their misgivings.

The child was unplanned, the result of one of Star's shrieks in the night. (She had finally found her father.) First, she decided, she would have to deal with that. Later that same day she would get out of town—in the afternoon, while Sebastian was at work. She would go in the clothes she stood up in, leaving everything behind but her jewellery, her best underwear stuffed into her shoulder bag.

"Have you got someone to take care of you when you get home?"

"Yes yes, I'll be fine."

And, she decided, she was going to get her hair buzz-cut. To hell with attracting men. They only brought trouble.

David's exhibition of paintings sold very well. So well that Star found herself on the night train to Sydney to negotiate a contract for his next exhibition with a gallery in Glebe.

"You go," David had said. "I'd only get ripped off. Crystal always said I was no good with money."

Doreen's affair with The Great Outdoors had crashed and burned like a jet on fire. She was sending David letters saying, "Remember our dream."

She was also sending him feathers.

Star was tired of waiting for the end, so she got on the Motorail. Doreen swept down from the hills as Star's train pulled away from the station. David allowed himself to be carried off. Feathers, paintings and all.

Star broke down. She lay in bed, swallowing anti-depressants. She could be reduced to tears by the smell of guttering candles.

Her father lay in the hospital bed. Tubes seemed to come out of every orifice.

It was winter. He was wearing Repatriation Hospital pyjamas and his old black-and-white beanie to keep his head warm. The dark hair Star remembered from her childhood had nearly all fallen out. There he lay, like a beaten knight on a battlefield. Stripped of his armour.

"Why don't you sing any more, girl?" he croaked at her. "You used to sing all the time around the house."

"What have I got to sing about, Dad?" she'd said. Bitter.

On the way home from the hospital, signs began to leap out at her:

TRESPASSERS WILL BE PROSECUTED

KEEP OUT. THIS MEANS YOU!

DEATH!! 40,000 VOLTS!

She went to a party the night before he died, bombed out on Valium and alcohol. Her mother stayed at the hospital, though her husband was unconscious. She sat in the ward, by his bed, knitting.

Waiting for him to die.

Twelve months after David's defection, Star was sitting in the back room of the Billinudgel Pub, drinking beer with Wayne, the business type who still fancied her. He kept asking Star back to his place in the mountains; she kept refusing. Then he happened to mention a foal he was raising.

"A foal?"

But Wayne had jumped up to play the jukebox and buy more beers; Star was broke, as usual.

The jukebox was playing "Tenderly", the Willie Nelson version, when David came in.

"I've split with Crystal," he said. "This is *it,* we're really finished this time."

"How'd you know where to find me?"

"I asked around."

Star ran her finger around the rim of her half-empty glass. Was it worth giving it another shot? David was patently unreliable, and she wanted children.

Wayne had moved away from the table. He was leaning against the jukebox in that ridiculously straight gear, looking stricken.

Star thought, as Willie Nelson's song headed for its conclusion. Wayne would probably be good with children. And there were horses. The kids would have a good life in the country.

She kissed David once.

"Tenderly . . ."

And left the pub with Wayne.

The late afternoon was clear and fine. A flock of white ibises perched like giant magnolias on an old tree near the railway line. They rose, screeching, as the south-bound Motorail went by and honked at the level crossing.

One long white feather spiralled down. Star walked over to it. Force of habit.

Then Wayne smiled and called to her from his SUV. He was waving bottles of Coca-Cola and bourbon.

She hesitated. David had come out on to the pub verandah. He looked confused.

She stepped over the feather in her dusty riding boots and got into the car with Wayne. They drove west.

She reviewed the events of her twenty-one years as they drove into the sunset. Thirty minutes into the mountains, just as the light was fading, Wayne turned down a dirt track. They passed a battered road sign that read: **NO THROUGH ROAD.**

3
Remains to be Seen

1987

The doorman at the Ex-Services Club won't let us in. "Sorry, sir," he says to Baby. "It's your T-shirt."

"My T-shirt?!"

Baby stands six-foot-four in fishnet stockings, so the doorman pretends to defer a bit.

"Today's the anniversary of the Battle of the Coral Sea," he goes on, little knowing the danger he's in. "There's a lot of the old fellows here tonight. They wouldn't like it; wouldn't like it one bit, that T-shirt."

"What's wrong with the bloody thing?" I ask like a man possessed. Beside me I can hear the psychic whine of Baby revving up to high gear.

"It's got a rising sun on it," the doorman explains patiently. "It looks Japanese. I can let *you* in," he points at me, "but not him. Not in that T-shirt. Sorry."

I drag Baby back to the parking lot and push him into

the car. As I ease the old Holden through the rain suddenly I can see, through the flashes of lightning, that the lot is filled with Japanese cars—Toyotas, Mitsubishis with bull bars—you name it, the place is full of them.

I slam my fist down on to the dashboard, but Baby just throws back his head and laughs. He seems to find it terribly amusing somehow.

He's still laughing as we drive through the slashing rain to David's with four six-packs.

This fucking rain, will it ever stop? I can see it through the open door of the chopper, though I can't hear it over the noise of the blades. We're the third drop into the landing zone, supposed to be a combined effort with the Americans, but the Marines won't go. I can hear the American CO on the radio threatening them with court martials and damnation, but they're not under his jurisdiction and they know it. They turn, all seven loads of them, and head back to where they came from.

So long, Marines, thanks a lot.

They're not so dumb: we're going straight down into an ambush. Looks like we're jumping right into the middle of the Vietcong's training field, and they've been planning for just such a contingency for months.

Across from me in the chopper Billy Boy's throwing up; he's green with fear—he's also Baby Johnson's kid brother. Baby's on R & R leave in Sydney. It's up to me to keep Billy Boy safe while he's away. Baby 'd probably frag me during a raid if I lost him.

The gunships hover above us, hosing down the edges of the clearing. They pull up and we're landing. Our door gunners let go one long burst and we run, heads down, for the trees.

The trees here are very different, unless you go right up into the mountains into rainforest country, and I don't like rainforests.

Not any more.

David's place is a cabin eight ks or so from the Mullumbimby post office. No power, but he runs a small generator when he can afford the petrol.

David makes a point of looking derelict and appearing cynical. I asked Baby one day why Dave was on the Disability Pension.

"Aw, he went mad when 'e turned nineteen," Baby said off-handedly. "Rather than taking him out an' shooting him, they put 'im on Stelazine instead. Long as he takes 'is medication he's fine."

"What happens if he doesn't take his medication?" I had to ask.

"He goes around talking to God and the angels. So they tell me anyway. Shit, how would I know?"

I'd looked at David more closely next time I saw him. He looked all right to me.

When we get to David's cabin, Bear's already there, sitting at the kitchen table staring moodily at a half-full bottle of rum, which doesn't please me particularly. Bear's bonkers. I know bonkers when I see it, and he's crazy. He's got thick, matted red hair down to his shoulders, a thick red beard, and when he's drunk he's mean and dangerous. You know when he's completely lost it: then he carries a hand hewn staff and puts flowers in his hair. There are no flowers tonight. I guess that's something.

I sit down at the kitchen table and rip open a beer. "Want one?" I ask David.

He sits down beside me on one of the torn vinyl chairs and peers at me through his government-issue glasses. "What's up, Michael?"

"Arr, nothing really. We got thrown out of the Ex-Services Club."

"Didn' even get in t' be thrown out," Baby adds from the depths of his Conan novel. Then he laughs as if he knows something I don't.

I get up and go into the bedroom section of David's one-room shack and look through his tapes and records. I figure if I don't get away from Baby I'll hit him.

The rain drums down on the old tin roof, Bear's off in some other space, which suits me fine, and as the night wears on David pulls two single mattresses off the bed in the kitchen and throws them on to the floor. He keeps them stacked there, all six of them one on top of the other, in case somebody wants a bed for the night. Sometimes I've arrived at seven on a winter's morning, and there's been six, maybe seven, people, some of them kids, sleeping on those mattresses in the kitchen. When you're the only person there at night and the mattresses are all stacked up, you need a chair to get on to the bed.

Bear says it reminds him of "The Princess and the Pea," which is a Hans Andersen fairy tale, I think. He tells David, from the lofty heights of the top mattress, that he can actually feel the pea and that *proves* that he's of royal blood, now doesn't it? But David doesn't understand the allusion at all—or so he says—while Baby and I pretend to be asleep.

It's twelve hours later. The radio won't work and we still can't find our unit. But we've been trained to work behind enemy lines. It's shithouse and you're scared all the time, but you'll get out if you stay cool, maintain discipline and keep a tight perimeter when you stop.

We move through the jungle in our Australian style, scouts well out front and back and on both flanks. Even the Americans admit we're the only people, apart from the VC, who know how to fight this fucking war and get good body counts for very few friendly KIA.

I walk down the line to see how Smithy's going, on my way encouraging Billy Boy, who's sobbing loudly. If I don't shut him up, he'll get us all killed. We can't make the time I'd like because Sebastian and Daddy Cool are carrying Smith under the shoulders, his legs dangling uselessly beneath him. He was hit before he even reached the tree line.

"You're doing fine, Smithy," I say to him, I've got this fucking routine off by heart. "Just a few more miles. You're gonna make it."

He opens his eyes and smiles at me. He knows I'm lying. His face is ashen from loss of blood. We've got no morphine, no medics; but he's an old NCO from WWII.

He doesn't make a sound.

When I wake up next morning, Baby's gone. David's ex,

Doreen (now calling herself Crystal), is sitting at the kitchen table, working her way through a flagon of port.

"Want some?" She smiles at me, flashing teeth and dreadlocks, the habitual blue heeler hide tied round her shoulders.

"What happened to the True Vine racket?" I say.

She hitches up close to me in case David's not as asleep as he seems. "The leader," she tells me. "We had a good thing going. Then he goes mental one night when I'm away at a workshop and crucifies himself on a big ironbark with lashings of barbed wire."

"Still alive?"

"Just. The followers came and fetched me when they found him in the morning. I took one look, then I tossed them the wire cutters and walked away. I might go back, I might not. Depends how I feel. We'll see."

I wonder how long she and David will last this time with their history of bitter brawls and rapturous reunions. Every time she leaves, David swears it's the end. Then she comes on like an advertising campaign, and the poor coot takes her back.

I get up and make myself a coffee, using the wood stove in the lean-to. Only David really understands the confusing collection of electrical cords fed by the generator, and he's still asleep, knocked cold by the Stelazine.

The coffee's good, sweet and black, the way I like it. David never has any milk, but there's always plenty of sugar. I stare into the bottom of the mug. What's a retired narc doing drifting around the far north coast of New South Wales, living on the Vets' Pension and hanging with what David affectionately calls "the low life"?

The bottom of the mug stares back at me. No answer.

I can hardly blame it on Azure.

I was working undercover as a bouncer in a nightclub in Kings Cross when I first saw her come in with six other people—Az is rarely alone; that's something I learned very early in my relationship with her. Getting Azure alone is tougher than having your teeth pulled.

But I also learned very early in the piece that she was a junkie and how she made the money to support her habit.

Classy, sure. But still . . .

She never tried to hide it from me. Azure doesn't know how to lie, she's like a child. Maybe it's because of her childlike quality that everyone loves her, and even the women don't hate her, in spite of her beauty. She was just nineteen when I met her, and within three months we were living together, she was clean and wasn't working any more, and I was the happiest guy in town.

I don't know what made me decide to return to the Northern Rivers. Maybe it was memories of my time here with the old man. Maybe it was getting shot in that bust on God. Maybe it was knowing that I had to get Azure out of Sydney if I was going to keep her clean. Whatever it was, I decided to quit the bureau. It took a year to make this happen, but in the end we had a garage sale one weekend and got on the train to Mullumbimby. Baby turned up soon after. *Cherchez la femme,* like they say—in his case, Star, the little hippy chick who'd lived next door to Az and me on the dunes in New Brighton. Baby's luck's holding—for now. But I wonder what'll happen when Wayne the Despicable's released from jail. Nothing ever works out for Baby. Everything he touches turns to trouble.

Azure and I were idyllically happy for a while, living near the sea on my retirement money, getting all-over tans and surfing every day. Then we moved to a farmhouse in the country, and the nightmares came back.

As the winter passed into the spring of that year and I couldn't find any work, we began to understand for the first time in our lives what it was like to be poor. Neither of us had ever lived below the poverty line before. It didn't take long to get to us.

Towards the end I started spending days at a time away, staying with Baby in his converted banana-packing shed in the mountains. Az and I were miserable all the time: we couldn't live together and we couldn't live apart. When it all finally exploded, neither of us had the slightest idea just what exactly it was that had gone wrong.

Who or what was to blame? We didn't know.

My RTO's got the radio working. I find we're about six ks from an American unit that's just digging in for the night. I talk to their G6 and tell him we're coming in from the south-east at around 1800 hours. I ask him to warn the men in that sector to watch out for us. Getting into an American unit after dark's just about the most dangerous manoeuvre you can execute. So many guys get blown away by trigger-happy friendlies.

We travel two ks without incident. Just as I'm beginning to think we're going to make it my tail scout tells me there's a full platoon of Vietcong, probably the NVA's 95th, all well geared up with AK47s, helmets, fatigues, the lot, coming up fast behind us.

I go back down the line to Smithy. While I'm weighing up what to do his eyes snap open and he says in a surprisingly clear voice, "Request permission to remain behind, sir."

The men watch me. The word's all down the line we've got an NVA platoon on our tail.

"What'd you have in mind, Top?" I say.

He tells me he wants us to prop him up against a tree off the track with all the grenades we can spare and extra ammo. I accede to this request and we push on faster now.

We haven't been gone from the spot fifteen minutes when I hear the first frags exploding behind us. There are some bursts of intermittent gunfire, mostly AK47s, then silence.

We tramp on. I pray Smithy made sure he wasn't taken alive. Beside me my corporal watches my face for some sign of emotion, but I don't have any emotion apart from that.

I'm just a robot with a mission.

Baby's in jail again. He went back and got the doorman after I fell asleep. He chose to go into Brunswick Heads lock-up, for word on the street has it that's the best place to work your fines off. He took in his portable record player, a swatch of vinyl records and a dozen Robert E Howard novels.

"You and those bloody Conan novels," I told him.

"You can laugh, y' bastard," he said. "I'd give anything to wake up one day in one of those Robert E Howard kingdoms. 'Stead of hanging around this shithouse planet."

We drive to Brunswick Heads to visit him in the afternoon, Azure and I, though we're still separated. At the last moment David and Doreen aka Crystal arrive. Rather than leaving them there to wreck the place—they're already well into the port and on the way to one of their innumerable arguments—we cram them in with us, flagons of port and all, and drive into Brunswick Heads.

We find Baby doing the police station's laundry at the laundromat down the road, drinking a can of Fosters and eating a pie as he aimlessly watches the dryers whirling around.

"Where're the cops?" asks Crystal Doreen, who has warrants out for her all over south-east Queensland and northern New South Wales.

"Aw, they're off duty, the place's all locked up. The sergeant's taken 'is wife down t' Ballina t' do 'er shopping."

"How are you going to get back in?" I ask him.

Baby looks sheepish. "Well, I can't. Not until they open the place at four."

"You mean you're locked out?! They've gone away and locked you out?"

"Get fucked, O'Neill."

"Want a snort of the port?" Crystal asks him. "It's in the car. Two flagons."

When Baby has got the laundry out of the dryers, we go back to the police station and lie on the front lawn in the sun, drinking port out of empty Coca-Cola bottles. It's a beautiful day. Little clouds are scudding across the sky, seagulls wheel overhead, and dimly in the distance you can hear the sound of the breakers smashing against the rock walls at the river's entrance.

I stare up into the sky and watch the seagulls, while

Crystal keeps on refilling the Coke bottles and the levels of the flagons in the car go down.

Up the path to the police station comes a little old lady carrying a straw basket and looking confused at finding the place locked up. Baby lurches off the lawn and lumbers across to her in his board shorts, tank top and thongs.

"Can I help ya, ma'am?"

"Oh, officer," she begins; she's mistaken him for an off-duty cop. I don't bother to listen to the rest, she's probably lost her cat or something, poor bitch, it'll only ruin my day.

Baby takes down all the details with a pencil and pad he's miraculously whipped out of his back pocket. He asks her to come back at four.

"So's the sergeant can see ya, ma'am."

"Thank you, officer," she smiles at him bravely. "You're very kind."

"Think nothin' of it, ma'am. That's what we're here for."

David and Crystal are fighting again, and the grog is running out. They say they'll go round to the Brunswick Pub and get some more, but I know they won't come back. They'll end up going nine rounds in Casuarina Park and throwing one another off the bridge to Main Beach. I don't care. It's good just lying here, listening to the drone of everyone's voices and watching Azure laugh. She laughs a lot, when she isn't crying.

I think a great deal about Azure and me that day. I wonder if it might've worked if we'd had more money, but there's a catch-22 in that. As long as Az is poor, she can't reacquire a habit. If she gets a job (and she's applied for one at the Top Pub back in town), she'll have the money to start again, and I won't be there to keep her on the rails.

The heat comes up out of the ground and soaks pleasantly through my body. I gaze up into the sky. My head is in Azure's lap and I'm not thinking straight—or maybe I'm thinking too straight. It'll be my birthday in five more days. In five days' time I'll be thirty-three. Half my life's gone, probably more; four combat wounds 've got to do something, and I don't mean something good.

What if we'd had a kid, Azure and I? She'd wanted one but I told her I was scared of the Agent Orange. Christ knows I saw enough of it, so that part's true. But the real truth of the matter is I don't want a kid. I lose my head completely every time the subject comes up.

What is it Kennedy said? "Ten per cent never get the word." We approach G company just as the light is fading. We come into their positions straight up the track as I had arranged with their American G6. The Vietcong are still on our tail and gaining, and all I want is to get my boys inside that friendly perimeter before nightfall.

The boys are tired and hungry. I go up and down the line, exhorting, threatening, cajoling—whatever it takes. Billy Boy's dry-eyed now. He's learned to cry inside like the rest of us. It hurts more but at least it doesn't make any noise.

I'm just coming back up to the front of the line when I see the flash. It's a light machine gun. I see the flashes from that one long burst as I hit the ground and roll to one side, yelling, "Foxes! Foxes! Shut off that fire!"

Behind me I see six of my men have fallen, some of them face-up, which means they're dead.

I rush up to the gunner's bunker, drag him out and knock him down. When he gets up I knock him down again, and I keep on doing that until he doesn't get up any more. No one in that American unit makes a move to stop me. They know he was asleep at the wheel and could've got them all killed during the night.

I go back to my boys. Three are dead, and Billy's lying so still I think he's gone too; but he isn't. Quite.

I kneel down beside him and hold him in my arms. He'll never make it.

"Did I—do—all right—sir?" he gasps.

"You did fine, Boy, just fine." I ruffle his hair.

I get to my feet, holding the empty Coca-Cola bottle, and tell Baby we're leaving, that we'll see him again tomorrow or the next day. Then Az and I drive back to what's billed on the highway as THE BIGGEST LITTLE TOWN IN AUSTRALIA. How many small towns, I wonder, have that sign at their entrance?

I drive the car over the railway line and park in the main street. As I get out of the car I see Bear in the distance. He's waving the hand hewn staff. He's got flowers in his hair.

I dash into the safety of the bottle shop and buy six bottles of Carrington champagne (it's on special). I nip next door when Bear's gone past and grab four week's worth of groceries off the shelves in record time. Then we head out to the farmhouse.

As we go over the third creek crossing Azure puts her hand on my knee and begins to stroke me. I figure we'd better talk now.

"What say we lock ourselves up in the house and don't come out for a month?" I ask her.

Silence. The wind whips Azure's hair in strands across her face. Long hair bleached blonde by the sun. We go through another creek crossing.

"A month?" She looks at me wonderingly with those clear grey eyes.

"Yep." I throw the car around the last bend, and the house looms up in front of us on the next hill. Good hill, that. From the top you can get a clear view of the terrain for three hundred and sixty degrees.

"I'd get—"

"Pregnant. Yes. I know."

Azure's laughing and hugging me. I take one hand off the wheel and ruffle her hair.

I'm going to start digging a fallout shelter next week. I'm going to buy bulk rations and ammunition and get more water tanks. This glasnost doesn't cut any ice with me. There's always some crazy bastard out there with his finger on a button.

"Are you quite sure?" Az is asking. "I mean, really?"

"I'm sure."

I drive the car over the cattle grid and slowly up the hill in first gear. I think I'm on the right track this time. But I guess that remains to be seen.

4
David's off his Meds

1987

I was waiting for her when she came out of the Chinese restaurant. I called to her from the shadow of the pile of lumber that stood beside the hardware store in the main side street of the small country town.

"What do you want?" She sounded frightened, as if talking to me was a crime for which someone might punish her, which was not so far from the truth now—who knows what those True Vine freaks get up to.

I just stood there. I heard the Motorail whistle at the level crossing that traversed the main street one block to the east of us. The Motorail whistled twice. Still, I didn't answer. I wanted to tell her I was going to save her, that I'd had a message, so clear, perfectly pure and beautiful, and that after tonight we'd be together again the way we used to be. But I couldn't say anything.

Crystal's eyes followed the line of hills to the west and

the little barred clouds. It was high summer, and although it was almost eight it was still daylight.

"Why don't you just go away and leave us alone? I don't owe you anything," she said.

The angel's wings were white. The angel's voice was golden. "I have a message from the Lord," he told me.

And here I am.

The track led downwards to the bottom of the valley, where the creek ran through it. As you approached the shack from the last hill all you could see was the roof, and the trees with the vines dangling from them. If the wood stove in the lean-to was lit, you'd see smoke drifting through the clearing.

Some nights I'd wake up beside Crystal in our shack in the valley. The moon would be shining through the branches, the dog would be lying before the dying wood stove with one eye open, and someone would be pounding on iron a long way up the creek. In those still nights I could almost feel the universe breathing. It was a good feeling.

The angel's hair was gold. The angel's sword was silver. "What God hath joined together, let no man put asunder," he told me.

Well, here I am.

They say I went crazy when she left me. I never believed them. Sure, I was upset but I wasn't crazy.

Her last words to me were, "You're nothing. You're no better than a dog!"

Every night after that I'd start drinking when the sun went down. Then I'd roam drunk around the multiple occupancy we shared with eight other families, howling, "*Nooo* better than a *dog!*"

I fell into the creeks, got covered in mud, scrabbling up the creek banks like The Creature from the Black Lagoon. The neighbours locked their doors and windows, which bothered me; I was just grieving. After twelve years she was everything to me.

It wasn't her fault, this break-up. *He* misled her. She was vulnerable and he knew it—everyone knew it; her so small and fine, looking fragile in her old St Vinnie's jeans. I should never have taken the job in Murwillumbah: gone at dawn, working twelve-hour days in the bananas six days a week. Come Sundays, I was no good for anything.

Now I know better. It'll be different next time.

The way I see it, she was lonely with me away all the time, and *he* was there. Yeah, he was there with his born-again rubbish. And I say to myself—I said it to myself again this morning when I saw them together in the main street—it's his *being there* that's the problem.

If he wasn't there, things'd be just like they used to be. We'd sit in front of the wood stove in the evenings with the kero lamps burning; listening to the radio, getting up before dawn. Christ, we had everything we wanted. She knows that, too; she just doesn't know how to get free of him. It's one of her failings: she's so gentle. She could never be cruel to anyone.

In the early days when I was desperate, I used to dream of burning him out. But there's no need for that; I see that now. I'm going round to his place tonight while she's at that *satori* workshop. I'm taking an iron bar and a rifle. I want to talk to this bloke, make him understand he's not important, that he just doesn't figure in the Grand Plan for her and me.

If he agrees to leave, I'll put him on the train to Sydney—no hard feelings. If he doesn't . . . well, I s'pose I'll think of something.

But I wanted to see her first to get up courage. Sometimes, I don't know, I get confused. Sometimes, you know, the vision falters. But I'm okay now; I've got it all thought out. When she gets up tomorrow, there'll be a surprise for her. Hey baby, the nightmare's over!

Christ, I love being married. Some people, they can't take it—all the ins and outs, the ups and downs. But when you love someone the way I love Crystal . . .

She depends on me. I won't let her down.

The angel's robe was silver. Was it my heart like lead that called him? "'Free her!' saith the Lord," he told me.

Lord, here I am.

5

Mr Lawson Regrets . . .

1995

Seven years in jail . . . Lawson aka God had ample time to reflect on how he'd gotten there, trace the paths that had led to this conclusion. Hard to believe, he thought, reconstructing the initial event at night in his cell, that it could lead to this.

He remembered stepping from the aircraft that fateful day, the tarmac soft under his feet. Christ, Central Australia was ghastly—just red soil, scrubby trees and dust. Why'd he taken this job?

Face it, Charlie, you were bored.

Yes, he'd been bored. Bored with his life in Sydney, his suburban life with Angela-and-the-kids, though he loved them. He'd jumped at the chance to get away for a while. Whatever else it might turn out to be, at least Maralinga would be a different kind of boring.

Lying on his bunk after lights-out, Lawson revisited his

first view of the Science Centre. So hi-tech for 1960, it loomed in the fierce sunlight as he crossed the tarmac from the plane to Reception, misgivings growing with every step.

As far as the eye could see, the facility was enclosed by a high fence topped with barbed wire. Armed guards patrolled the fences. And all this security was for what? So the Brits could play with a few bombs.

At the entrance he paused, took the crumpled telegram from his pocket, smoothed it out and read it again:

> ***Come to Maralinga STOP Will make it worth your while STOP***
>
> ***Richard Hall***

Lawson hoped Hall would make it worth his while. Middle-aged academics with expensive tastes needed all the lucre they could get. He took one last look at the landscape and stepped inside into the welcome cool.

The Centre's vestibule was deserted except for the guards on the doors. So much security, Lawson thought. As if anyone in their right minds was going to come out here unless you paid them. He dumped his bags, went over to the reception desk and leaned on the buzzer.

No one came.

The vestibule was full of armchairs and coffee tables—no sofas. Lawson sat down in a club chair near the fake waterfall, leaned his head on his arms and tried to breathe through his post-flight nausea. It had been a rough flight in a Fokker Friendship, air pockets all the way from Sydney.

Just as he was beginning to pass out, a young man in his early twenties came into the room through one of the internal doors. He was wearing a khaki uniform and boots. His hair had been dyed a beautiful shade of platinum. He had green eyes.

"Why didn't you buzz?" this apparition demanded.

Lawson had a sudden memory of wanting to become invisible at will. He'd been eight at the time, spending his pocket money on fake ink blots bought off the back pages of comic books, skeletons on strings, watches with luminous hands and dials ***(Read in the dark. A marvel!)***, fake dog turds . . . If only he'd known. All you had to do was dye your hair grey. Grey hair would render you invisible.

Lawson bestirred himself, patted at that iron-grey hair—should he have dyed it?

"Thanks for the welcome. It's touching."

The young man's eyes flashed. Lawson got the feeling they weren't going to get on.

"You," he said, and Lawson didn't like the way he said the word, "must be Charles Doyle."

"*Professor* Charles Doyle," he replied, but his ID didn't seem to impress the platinum-haired stranger.

Lawson studied the young man from under the brim of his Akubra hat, bought especially for the occasion. His days of chasing young men were gone. Besides, this one was *too* young—and far too beautiful.

And the longer he stayed, Lawson thought, the better looking the boy would get.

"Richard Hall?" he asked. "Is he in?"

The young man gave a frosty smile. "This way please," was all he said.

They tramped down endless corridors like characters in *Last Year at Marienbad*, Lawson trailing behind with his bags while the young man strode lightly on ahead. At one stage he became lost, the boy was so far ahead, and a tall man with dark hair, horn-rimmed glasses and eyes like a horse that had been through a fire came along and tried to induce Lawson to view his fungus.

Then the young man came back and rescued him grudgingly, cutting short the pathetic, wild-eyed scientist, leaving Lawson unceremoniously outside Richard Hall's door.

Hall was just as Lawson remembered him from university days: big and blond, with a broken nose from a football brawl. Lawson liked him a lot. But Hall had hung up his boots long ago and married Nancy. Really married, Lawson thought, the full catastrophe. Pipe and slippers stuff.

They embraced in the awkward fashion of men.

"How long has it been?"

Lawson sat down in a leather armchair and lit up a Sobranie cigarette. "Don't ask."

"Still smoking those things?" Hall asked. "They'll kill you. The research is in. So far the tobacco companies are managing to keep it quiet."

"The boy with the platinum hair," Lawson said. "Who's he?"

"Jamie? He's my chief archaeologist. Best archaeologist I've had in a long time. Leave him alone."

"What's his name?"

"Shit, Charlie, you just got here. His name's Stanborough. James Stanborough." Hall had begun his routine with the pipe, a routine familiar to Lawson from their student days. "Did he meet your flight? I thought he was organising a staff meeting on Level 1."

"And the Fungi Man?"

"Anson Blake? He's all right. Quite harmless."

Lawson gazed through the window at the desert. This was red dirt country. Small whirlwinds of dust drifted along the horizon. An explosion far in the distance sent a miniature mushroom cloud into the air. For a while it hung there, looking like a smaller version of what he'd seen in the newsreels, until the wind began to disperse it slowly southwards.

"That stuff," Lawson said, "the fallout. What happens to the people downwind?"

Hall frowned. "Oh you mean the indigenous population. They were moved off at the beginning of the project and warned to stay away."

"I saw some camped to the south of here when I flew in."

"It's not my department, Charlie. I'm just here for the dig. The Brits are responsible for the rest." Hall waved a hand towards the slowly dispersing mushroom cloud. "You have to understand, resources are limited. My concern is this." He opened the top drawer of his desk and handed Lawson a small object wrapped in waxed paper. "What do you make of it?"

Lawson unwrapped the coin and turned it over in his hands. It looked ancient, but he knew from years of investigating frauds that looks didn't mean anything. Holding the coin, he found himself thinking of James Stanborough's hair and wondered at the connection.

"Is it one those medieval African coins?" Hall was saying. "You know, like the ones found at Marchinbar Island back in 1944?"

Lawson went over to the window and held the coin this way and that to the light. "Sorry. Nothing like."

"Indigenous Australian?"

"They're nomads, for Christ's sake."

"Space visitors?"

"You're scraping the bottom of the barrel. Where'd you find it?"

"About twenty-five ks north of here. Sector 5. But there's very little to see, I'm afraid," Hall added in the Now-There-Everything'll-Be-All-Right voice Lawson knew he saved for difficult situations.

"Okay, Rich," Lawson said. "What happened?" He placed the coin on the desk and sat back down in the fine old leather armchair. "You can give it to me straight, without the marshmallows."

"We blew up the site."

Lawson removed his spectacles and began polishing them to hide his displeasure. He was a man who didn't like to show his feelings.

"It was just another explosion site to the Brits." Hall puffed on the pipe. "Nothing atomic. They were experimenting with army clothing and various kinds of explosives. When they went in later to check the dummies, they found this," he held up the coin, "buried among the rubble. Before you get too excited, though, there's nothing there."

"Metal detectors?"

"Don't register anything. All we've got is this one coin. I faxed copies to the best numismatists in the West. It's nothing they've ever seen. I'm running out of experts fast, that's why I sent for you. I need to know if this find is genuine. I can't keep the lid on it forever."

Through the window Lawson could see the desert night coming down and, though it was warm in the room, he shivered. "No bones, no charcoal, nothing organic associated with it?" He was thinking of radiocarbon dating. It was reliable, with correction curves, up to forty thousand years. But it worked only on carbon-based life forms—wood, plants, animals.

Hall shook his head. "Sorry. I've given you a whole laboratory on Level 3. Offhand though, your thoughts."

Lawson ashed out his cigarette. "Are you sure no one from the Centre could've brought it here when they came?"

"You think it's fake."

Lawson could hear the disappointment in his old friend's voice. "It's just a thought."

Hall shook his head. "I don't see how anyone could've brought it in. Every item that comes into this place is screened."

True, Lawson reflected. He'd been everything short of cavity searched before he boarded the plane in Sydney.

Somewhere a bell sounded. It seemed a long way away. Hall wrapped the coin back up in the waxed paper and returned it to the top drawer of the oak desk.

"Dinner," he said.

As they were leaving the room Lawson hesitated. "Don't you think that coin should be kept in a safe or something?"

"Who from?" Hall asked, half-impatient, half-amused. "They've run intensive security checks on everyone here. Even you." He glanced out the window at the gathering dusk. "And there are no spacemen here. Haven't been for quite a while."

If there ever were at all, Lawson thought.

The morning came up grey to match his mood. Lawson clad himself in his Akubra and khaki work issue and went down in the lift to the basement to meet his crew. He felt uneasy; he didn't know why.

After he'd been introduced to the dig crew, fifteen men in all, they fixed their hats, climbed into four-wheel-drives and set off for the site, the last jeep trailing their equipment.

After an hour of jolting, an hour that seemed like an eternity to the urbane Lawson, they approached the site. It was just another version of desolation as far as he was concerned.

He found Kingston, the foreman of the dig team, and said, "Unload the gear—and I want the fellow who found the coin to come with me."

Kingston grinned broadly and pointed to James, who stepped forward and said coldly, "I'm the one who found it, *Professor* Doyle."

"Charles will do," Lawson told him. "And okay, *you* come with me."

They set off together across the rubble, leaving the team behind them unloading bags of tools and boxes of equipment and joking with one another. Their camaraderie made a heavy contrast to the studied indifference that passed between Lawson and Stanborough.

Fifty metres ahead of them, Lawson saw what appeared to be a well-organised dig. He'd been hoping to find something wrong when he inspected it, but everything was in order.

"What depth are you down to?" he asked Stanborough.

"Ten metres."

Still they'd come up with nothing.

"Perhaps," Lawson said, "we're digging in the wrong place. Perhaps the coin was flung here by the force of the blast."

"I didn't dig where the coin was found," James said shortly. "I dug at the centre point of the blast. Ground zero."

Lawson regrouped. "Good, that's good. Go tell Kingston I want him, please."

Stanborough turned without a word and went off to relay Lawson's instructions, still stylish, even in regulation khaki.

Lawson climbed up on to one of the mounds of rubble and surveyed the scene in every direction. Somewhere under this area might be proof that early Australian history was not what they'd thought—or was the whole thing an elaborate hoax? As for the boy, he thought to himself, watching Stanborough's retreating form, forget it. This is not an Alan Ladd movie where they fall into one another's arms at the end.

For the best part of a week Lawson stayed back at the base, setting up his laboratory and planning his attack on the coin, while Stanborough and the team dug on. Every time he picked up the coin he felt uneasy, and that was bad, for he had learned to trust his intuition. He was the best troubleshooter in the business when it came to numismatic fraud. There were many people, some in surprisingly high academic places, whose bids for fame had come unstuck because of the results from his laboratory.

During all his years in the business he never used an assistant and he always locked his laboratory doors. You might say he was cynical by nature.

Stanborough was on his mind, but the only time Lawson got to see him was in the evenings in the main dining hall. The boy (Lawson couldn't help thinking of him as a boy) usually sat with Anson Blake at a small table in one corner. Blake was obviously besotted with him and, watching them sometimes, Lawson almost felt sorry for the fungi man—almost, but not quite. There was something about Blake he didn't like.

Like the coin, he made Lawson feel uneasy.

As an expert on fraud, Lawson was used to a certain amount of adulation, but as time went on Stanborough remained unimpressed. When Lawson discovered that a chemical he needed for tests was missing from his laboratory and would take five days to replace, he went down to the basement one morning and informed Stanborough that the two of them were going to crosscheck the metal detector readings on the entire site.

Stanborough was peeved. "Can't you get somebody else?"

"No," Lawson lied.

He managed to drag out the five days to six. They hiked with detectors and notebooks and ignored one another, while the sun blazed down and the team dug on good-humouredly, always hoping they might strike it lucky, become a part of scientific history.

Personally, Lawson doubted that. He doubted it very much.

When two people work together in the field, they get to

know one another, even if they don't talk a lot. Just as he'd hoped, Lawson got to know Stanborough, and the more he did, the more he realised that what he had first interpreted as cool was really a defence, a kind of structure James had erected to cover his fear. Lawson found himself wondering if the young man had been ill-treated in some way in the past. He had a childlike quality to him that sometimes flashed out suddenly and made Lawson want to protect him.

But hey, Lawson thought, lying on his bed in Grafton jail, there's no fool like an old fool.

When he and Stanborough had finished the metal detector runs, they worked around the dig with the team. One particular day there was a feeling of something in the air, so Lawson hung close to the excavation. Sure enough, late in the afternoon, minutes before the crew was due to leave for base, there was a shout from Kingston, who'd been sieving rubble six metres below the surface.

Everyone crowded around and there it was: coin no. 2, identical in almost every respect to no. 1, definitely from a similar era.

The members of the team were jubilant. They stacked their gear in record time, piled into their jeeps and raced one another back to base and the bar. Stanborough and Lawson remained behind to examine the new specimen under the portable electron microscope. After half an hour they climbed into their vehicle and headed for home.

Lawson drove over the parched red landscape with mixed feelings: two coins didn't mean any more than one, unless they were genuine.

Ahead of them stood an ancient cliff, its base pitted with caves of varying sizes. They drove past it every day on their way to and from the dig. Just as they drew level with this cliff, their jeep stopped and wouldn't start again. They got out and worked it over. The engine had seized.

They were stranded.

Stanborough began unloading packs from the back of the vehicle. "Here," he said, shoving the largest pack into Lawson's arms, "we've got to get inside and get things organised before the cold sets in."

"What's this?" Lawson asked, staggering under the weight of the pack.

"It's sleeping bags, and tinned food and lights, things like that. It's standard regulation equipment on all vehicles."

"Surely they'll send someone out for us."

Stanborough shrugged. "*If* we're missed," he said. "Come on. Night's coming down, we've got to hurry."

Already the visibility was fading. Lawson slung the pack over his back and trudged after Stanborough. It was possible, he thought, that they might not be missed. There were two bars and two dining halls in the Centre, and an unwritten code that no one ever bothered you in your room. They might ring, but if you didn't answer, they'd leave you alone.

They reached the entrance to the largest cave, took the torches from their belts and stepped inside into the gloom. The cave had the air of an abandoned camp. The level floor was scattered with boulders of differing sizes. The walls rose up to form a cathedral-like ceiling ten metres above their heads. Here and there on one section of the walls were hand prints in ochre, relics of the people who'd roamed there long ago.

The cold was setting in as the two men set up lights, unpacked gear and got out the emergency rations. As Lawson worked at this he couldn't help wondering at the change in Stanborough. For weeks he'd hardly given Lawson the time of day. Now he was stuck in the middle of nowhere with him, he behaved like a kid at a birthday party.

"Look!" he exclaimed, holding up the last item for Lawson's inspection. "Brandy."

It was, too. A whole bottle of it.

"Is that so we won't notice we're freezing to death?"

"Come on, Charles, it never goes below minus five."

But Lawson had a horror of the cold. He'd been born on the coldest day in Sydney for fifty years. Cold was his mortal enemy. His house in Sydney was air-conditioned at a time when air conditioning was rare. He had a fireplace in his living room and lit a fire every night through the winter.

He dug through the bundles they had brought inside. Among all the high-tech objects, no one had thought to include a box of matches. "Do you smoke?" he asked Stanborough. But Lawson already knew that he didn't.

The night came down, and with it came the cold. The two men sat side by side (Lawson shivering in front of the battery-operated air heater, and wishing for a fire), eating emergency rations and socking down the brandy.

"Drink up!" Stanborough refilled his mug. "Here's to fame and money—*lots* of money!"

Lawson barely answered. Something was bothering him. It stalked the back lanes of his mind like an assassin in a fog. He sat on a rolled-up sleeping bag and thought: even inside the cave with the air heater and their sleeping bags and the brandy, he was in for a very uncomfortable night.

The heater gave one desperate splutter and died.

Lawson turned to Stanborough. "Has anyone ever survived this?"

"Kingston and Boyle got caught out six weeks ago," James said. His hair had taken on a silver tint under the emergency lights.

Well, Lawson thought, Kingston was still breathing, but he'd never heard of anyone called Boyle. Maybe Boyle had seen the light and caught the next stage out of town.

"I don't suppose their heater died."

"Actually, it did," James replied. "But they put their sleeping bags together."

They were out of brandy. Suddenly they seemed to be out of talk as well. James looked at Lawson, then he zipped the two sleeping bags together and they crawled into them.

"Goodnight," Lawson said and turned his back to Stanborough.

The walls loomed eerily in the half-dimmed battery lights. The hand prints of people long gone added to the sense of desolation. Lawson felt very alone and a long way from home.

And then a strange thing happened: Stanborough kissed him on the nape of the neck as Lawson lay with his back to him.

"Go to sleep," Lawson told him. "You're drunk. You'll regret it in the morning." He was determined he wouldn't touch the young man. He had a bad feeling about him.

For what felt like hours, he lay like a stone while Stanborough stroked his hair and covered his neck with soft kisses. If he'd made even one crass move, Lawson might've saved himself, but he didn't. Eventually Lawson's caution so long held deserted him, and he allowed James to undress him.

James took him in his arms. It felt like coming home. When they touched, they seemed to blend and blend. For once in his life Lawson trusted. He found the timeless ocean and drowned without regret.

At first light next day a rescue team, alerted by their absence at the morning mustering point, found them and took them back to base. Lawson spent the drive trying to figure out who'd sabotaged his jeep.

Someone had.

In a small community news travels fast.

"Congratulations on the second find," Hall said, when he met Lawson in the dining hall that evening. "But be careful, Charlie, won't you?"

Even Anson Blake came up and shook Lawson's hand with a weird smile—an experience Lawson could well have done without.

There followed one of the happiest periods of Lawson's life. By day he worked in his laboratory while James supervised the dig, and at night they spent the evenings together in his room.

In every relationship, even the failed ones, there are things you remember, tapes you replay. Until the day he died, Lawson only had to close his eyes and he'd be back there.

They'd been lying in bed together in James's room, fooling around. Suddenly James jumped off the bed and pretended to run away from him.

"You'll get tired of me," he protested. "I know you, Charles Doyle—you're fickle."

Fickle. Ah yes, Lawson thought, that was him. With his cats, his TV guide and Angela-and-the-kids; his oh so predictable life that was choking him.

He pursued James and pinned him against the wall near the antique mirror.

"I'm not fickle," he said. "Well, not any more anyway."

James looked up into his face like a child. "Truly?" he whispered.

Lawson pushed a lock of platinum hair out of the younger man's eyes. "Truly." A rush of something he'd never felt before came over him. He wanted to say *I love you,* for the first time in his life. Instead, he touched James' hair.

And after that they didn't speak at all.

Had Lawson been working fifty years later, a whole range of technologies would have been available to him, but in 1960, analysing metal finds from archaeological digs was a time-consuming process involving chemical analyses of minute pieces of the coin itself. Lawson didn't mind; he excelled in this area that other people found boring. He liked having a concrete problem with a concrete solution. The benches, the apparatus, the routine—even the problem itself—was solid and real. He liked that.

And yet . . .

Why did he feel so uneasy? There was no doubt that he and James were in line for the prestigious Watson Award and, if Lawson could give James proof of authenticity to support his find, they'd both be famous. And rich. Lawson already had a certain degree of fame, but the money would mean no more crawling to academic boards for funding.

He worked his way through the tests with nothing coming out clearly one way or the other. It was like finding that second coin when the metal detector runs he'd done with James had registered negative. Nothing checked out.

Finally he approached the only test he had left. For this, a larger sample of alloy needed to be obtained from the coin, so he had kept it until last. He mixed up the necessary reagents with scrapings from the first coin, placed the Erlenmeyer flask on the asbestos mat and lit the Bunsen burner.

These primitive processes, he thought. It was like being back in the Middle Ages.

After the solution came to the boil, he'd have twenty minutes to wait for his result, and this one would be conclusive. If the solution turned green, the coin was of recent origin. If it turned red, it was authentic. The problem of its place of origin would still remain, but Lawson would cross that bridge when he came to it. *If,* he thought to himself, he ever did.

He sat down to wait on one of the tall laboratory stools. He felt restless and almost wished he were back on the site, though by now he was convinced there was nothing to find and that this last test would prove the coins to be a brilliant attempt at fraud.

After five minutes the solution came to the boil, and Lawson lowered the flame on the Bunsen burner. He couldn't handle his feelings any longer, just sitting there, so he locked his laboratory and went for a stroll on Level 3. He had a quarter of an hour to kill. The door to the Personnel Records room was open, so he ambled in, thinking to pass the time with the office workers, but the place was empty.

Lawson surmised the workers had gone to morning tea. Opportunity knocks but once, he told himself. He walked over to the four-drawer filing cabinet and searched through the folders for the one marked STANBOROUGH, JAMES—just why, he didn't know. Maybe he doubted James's story; he wouldn't have been the first person in history to have embroidered a little on the truth. But it was all there, just the way he'd told it: the drunken father, the poverty, the abuse, the scholarship that saved him from the streets.

On an impulse Lawson looked up BLAKE, ANSON, but he found nothing there of any note. Only Blake's qualifications were unusual: first botanist Lawson had ever met who'd begun his career in engineering, then switched over to botany later on.

He was about to search through the folders for DOYLE, CHARLES—which would've made interesting reading, he didn't think—when he heard the workers coming back along the corridor. He didn't stay to talk. The time for the conclusion of his experiment was almost up, and the timing was critical.

He returned to his laboratory to find Blake standing just outside his door, looking shifty. He hadn't seen much of Blake in the past few weeks, since he and James got together, in fact. He'd heard Blake worked strange hours at night in his room, as if he were The Invisible Man or something, but as long as Lawson didn't have to see him, that was all right by him.

Now, seeing Blake standing there outside the locked

door of his laboratory, fishing about in the pockets of his lab coat, Lawson realised with a shock how much he hated him.

"Have you got any spare Caustic Soda?" Blake asked in his nasal voice, explaining that he had run out. Lawson made him stand outside the lab while he fetched it, and Blake went off thanking him too profusely.

Lawson locked the door when Blake had gone and tried to shake off the feeling the botanist always evoked in him. To hell with Blake, he thought. And what if the coins *are* a fraud, so bloody what? For once in his life, he had something that mattered more.

He hurried on down between the laboratory benches to where the Erlenmeyer flask sat simmering gently on the tripod. To his utter amazement the solution was red—not green, as he had expected, but red.

The coin was genuine.

Within hours it was all over the base that the coins were genuine. Hall doubled the strength of the team working on the dig, and Lawson and Stanborough sat down to write the paper that would win them the Watson Award, given annually for a significant find in archaeology.

Still, Lawson remained uneasy. Why were there no other artefacts of any kind? He repeated the critical test, using scrapings from the second coin, but the results tallied with what he'd obtained before.

Yet his unease persisted. It was still there on the night before his return to Sydney. He was leaving by light plane in the early morning, but Jamie was to remain until the site search was finished.

The night before he left for Sydney, Lawson went back to his room early while the celebrations over the find were still in progress. He didn't go straight to Jamie's room; he didn't want to. He felt alone somehow and terribly exposed. Success had always had that effect on him.

He lay on his bed and stared at the ceiling, trying to figure out where the technology that had produced the coins could've come from. And all the while his sense of unease continued.

Eventually he got up and went around the corridor to James's room. Blake's lights were on, his door was open, and Lawson realised then that Blake's bedroom was next to Jamie's, something that hadn't registered with him before.

As he drew level he stopped and looked in through the botanist's open door. It was a strange sight: Blake had the radio on, and he was doing a little jig between the bed and the writing desk, stopping every now and then to refill his champagne glass from the bottle in the ice bucket and to swallow a few more gulps.

"Well thanks," Lawson said. "I didn't know you cared." And, without being invited, he stepped inside.

Then he realised Blake was watching a film of some kind.

The image Lawson saw was projected on to the opposite wall of Blake's bedroom, the wall not visible from the corridor. Blake moved quickly to switch off the reel, but it was too late. Even in that split second Lawson *knew* that platinum hair.

He pushed Blake as he moved towards the projector. Blake stumbled. His finger hit the *Pause* button instead of *Off*, and there was James in front of Lawson on the bed, hair glowing like molten metal, the night Lawson almost said, I love you.

Lawson's knees went from under him. He dropped into a chair between Blake and the door.

"How did you get this?" he croaked. His voice didn't seem to belong to him.

Blake pointed to the wall of his bedroom, the wall that adjoined Stanborough's. "You always did admire Jamie's antique mirror. Quite taken with it, you were." He walked over to the desk and poured himself another glass of champagne. "Would you like a drink? It's a very fine vintage, I had it flown up weeks ago for the occasion."

The *Pause* button on the projector was faulty. It lifted off, and the reel continued to play. The picture changed, and there was James on Blake's bed in the same pose, hair falling across his face like molten silver.

Only this time, Lawson saw with a lurch that Blake was . . . with him.

"Would you like the soundtrack?" Blake hissed jubilantly; he seemed like a different person. "I'll turn off the radio so you can hear better. Ah, don't you just adore it when he's vulgar?"

Lawson made it out of the chair. He grabbed Blake and shoved him backwards against the wall. Blake was a weed, and Lawson was still strong. All those chores on his father's dairy farm had given him a good start.

"You were inventive, Doyle," Blake was saying as the images thrown by the projector continued to play over both of them. "I'll give you that. There were a couple of things you missed, though. Personal taste, I suppose. Do you know what he likes most of all?" He leered into Lawson's face, no glasses now. "He likes being beaten first—but I notice that's not your style."

Lawson released Blake and turned to go. He was afraid if he hit him just once, he'd never stop.

"Hey!" Blake called after him. "What are you doing tonight, Lawson? How about we make a threesome of it?"

Lawson strode back into the room and punched Blake. The botanist fell heavily against a chest of drawers and lay still. For a moment, Lawson thought Blake's neck was broken, but he was simply unconscious. Which probably saved his life.

Lawson stepped out into the corridor and went to James's room. James was wearing green silk pyjamas that matched his eyes. He put his arms around Lawson when he opened the door.

"Hi, Sweetie."

Lawson shoved him away. "I've just been to see Blake," he said in the voice that didn't belong to him. "Why did you do it—*why?*"

"Listen, Charlie," James said, urgent now. "The paper's written. You'll be ruined if you go back on it now. Think for a moment, we can all be rich!"

Lawson couldn't follow him. He just stood there. All he could see in his mind was that picture of James with Blake.

"The results," he heard himself saying. "People are depending on us."

"Oh, stop talking like the White Knight of the academic world, Charles Doyle," James said. "What does any of this matter? I mean to say, *who cares*?"

Then Lawson got it. "Give me the duplicate key Anson made to my laboratory."

Anson Blake, Batchelor of Engineering & Metalurgy.

James took the key from his desk drawer and handed it to him without a word.

"You stole my key and gave it to him to copy so he could fix my results." Now the rage was mounting in Lawson. "You planted those coins. Does money mean *that much* to you?"

And, God forgive me, Lawson thought, shifting uncomfortably on the narrow jail bed, I hit him.

James fell to the floor without a sound and crawled across the carpet to where Lawson stood in his horror. What happened after that—or, rather, what almost happened—Lawson would never reveal to anyone.

He lifted the younger man to his feet and looked into his eyes at the scars that would never go away. "Oh, little one," he said.

James didn't speak.

Lawson tightened his arms around him. "You can leave him. You can come with me."

James shook his head. Then he put his arms around Lawson in that childlike way he had and kissed him.

Lawson closed his eyes and felt it one last time, that feeling of belonging. Gone forever. Then he put James away from him.

"Don't do it, Charlie. You'll be ruined if you do!" James shouted as Lawson left the room, slamming the door behind him.

Lawson walked through the corridors for a long time. He knew the damage to his reputation would be immense if he spoke up. His affair with James would become an academic scandal. He'd probably be asked to leave the university. Perhaps he should change direction; he was a good chemist.

He'd gotten away from the dairy farm. Maybe, just maybe, he could get away from this . . .

Lawson rolled over on his cell bed. He checked his watch. The screws would be by soon, rousting everyone up for the day.

Well, you did speak up, Charlie, old boy. Eventually. The sun was rising and the Centre was stirring by the time you knocked on Richard Hall's door. And you did change direction. From Charles Doyle, respected professor of chemistry, to Charles Lawson, the biggest manufacturer of heroin on the Far North Coast. Can't blame anyone but yourself for that.

The door to Lawson's cell clanked open. A guard stood there.

"Get up, old man, you're free—you and your scumbag mate Abrahams."

6

So long, Baby

1995

She can hear his footsteps on the concrete path that runs along the side of the house. It's eight at night. The children are watching TV.

Now he's banging on the back door, and Star's not looking forward to the visit.

She unlocks the door and Baby pushes past her. He's carrying a shotgun in one hand and a bottle of Beenleigh rum in the other.

"You're going back to Wayne now he's out—aren't you?"

She says Yes. There's no point in denying it; this is a small town.

"Where're the kids?" he asks her.

"Watching TV."

"Good," Baby says, "I don't want them to see this. Come in here."

He pulls her into her bedroom at the back of the house

and bolts the door. The barrel bolt is the one he put on himself when he was living with them.

"I've been thinking," he says, "and I've decided to shoot you. After that I'm going to go looking for Wayne and shoot him too."

"Are you going to shoot yourself as well?" she asks.

Baby takes a long swig of rum from the bottle. "Nah, you're not worth it."

Star reaches for the bottle where he's put it down on the bedside table. He pulls it away so that she can't reach it.

"Wayne's in Brisbane at the moment," she says, her mean streak coming out, "and you don't know where he's staying."

"I'll find him."

She tries a different tack. "You can't shoot me. What about the children?"

Baby looks horrified. "Christ, I wouldn't touch them—what kind of a person do you think I am! I've taken a card of Serepax." He tosses the empty card on to the washstand. "Now I'm going to drink this whole bottle of rum—"

She makes another pass at the bottle as he holds it up. He fends her off.

"So, in the morning, I won't remember anything," he says triumphantly. "No remorse. Nothing."

Star doesn't like this. He's given the matter too much thought. "Give me a drink, Bobby, c'mon—you've got a whole bottle there, you can spare it."

Baby holds the bottle behind his back. "Nope."

"Who else but you," she says, "would come here with a bottle of rum, tell me they're going to shoot me, and not even give me a drink? You know I love rum and I can't afford it. No wonder I left you, you're selfish!"

Not true. Star left Baby because he stopped taking his medication for post-traumatic stress disorder. She couldn't handle him when he was off it. Then he drank too much and fell into terrible depressions that dragged her down. She couldn't afford to go down. If she did, what would become of the children?

Baby leans the shotgun against the wall. She can tell by the way he does this that it is loaded.

"Oh all right," he says. "I suppose you can have a drink, seeing as I'm going to shoot you."

He passes her the bottle with a certain grudging deference, and she realises then that he's going to do it. She's going to be blown away.

She gets into her bed and props herself up with pillows. She figures she might as well make herself comfortable. As she sits there drinking, a soft powerful energy seems to flow into the room, and the quality of the light seems different.

Everything becomes clear and beautiful: the yellow rose in the china cup on the washstand, the white candle burning in the little brass candlestick her eldest son gave her last Mother's Day, her pale blue curtains, long to the floor, such a soft, soft blue.

In the other room her children are laughing at something on TV. Beautiful beyond belief is the sound of their laughter. The only thing that isn't beautiful is Baby's grief, which Star can't save him from. She feels sad, to the point of tears, about that.

She passes the bottle of rum back to him. He drinks from it, then sets it down on the old washstand.

"Bobby," she says to him, "I'm only going back to Wayne

because of the children."

Baby hands her the bottle again; she can't reach it from where she sits in her bed. The rum tastes good. She doesn't think she's ever felt better in her life, except that she feels sad for Baby, and for everyone else who ever lost someone dear to them.

"Please take me back, Star, I won't be any trouble. I'll take my medication and I won't rave." He's pacing around the foot of her bed, first one way, then the other. He's not so steady on his feet any more.

"I'm sorry," she says. She's thinking how kind he's always been to her and the children—how kind he's been to everyone, in fact.

And how little rewarded.

Eventually there's no rum left in the bottle, Baby's smoked all his cigarettes, and when he walks he staggers.

"Please Star," he says to her again, stumbling as he comes around the foot of her bed.

She thinks of those first fine years, then she says No.

"Kiss me goodbye," he says, crying.

She does.

"Why didn't you love me, Star?" he says as he pulls away. "Oh, why did you stop loving me?"

She's got no answers. Not for that. Not for anything.

Then he goes away, leaving the shotgun leaning against the wall. She can hear his footsteps stumbling along the concrete path beside the house. Then the front gate slams.

She unloads the shotgun and locks it in the wardrobe. In the living room the children switch off the TV. Her eldest son puts his head around the door.

"Goodnight, Mum."

Her youngest comes in and crawls into bed with her; he's only nine. "Can I sleep with you tonight?"

"Sure you can, darling. Sure you can."

Baby's footsteps have died away. As Star locks the back door she hears his car start up. Tomorrow, she thinks, she'll start to pack, move back into Wayne's house in Mullumbimby.

Beyond the dunes, the sea is roaring like an express train.

7
Stella by Starlight

2002

It's hard to adjust to adjust to poverty when you've been a big wheel most of your life. Lawson made the best of it when he was released from jail, setting himself up with the help of St Vincent de Paul in a cheap, two-storey unit near the beach in the northernmost suburb of Byron Shire. It was a suburb so neglected (no streetlights, no footpaths and very few buses) he could well have been living on an island. Which suited Lawson just fine.

On the day he planned to kill himself, the day he'd decided had the best chance of success, he rose at six as usual.

"Come on, Cynthia, time to get up."

The old cat had slept all night on the end of the bed. Now she stretched and rose reluctantly. Lawson leaned over to pat her.

"Where's Bruiser, Cynthia? Where's that young hulk?"

Charles Lawson pulled on cotton slacks and a shirt, put on his spectacles and ran a comb through his white hair without looking into the mirror. He had no use for mirrors any more. In the kitchen he opened the back door and called for the young cat.

"Bruiser! Yoohoo, Bruiser!"

When the young cat came in, spruce and self-important on the third call, he rushed straight to his bowls and began to wolf down the food. Charles Lawson watched him as he ate. This was his first summer and, although neutered, he'd taken to staying out in the evenings, which caused Lawson much anguish of spirit as he watched the clock through the night.

When the cats had been fed, he made himself a cup of freshly ground coffee with a generous dash of whipping cream and two sugars. Every nutrition book he'd ever read put coffee down, but since he'd decided on his Course of Action, as he called it, he didn't see the point any more in depriving himself of this small pleasure.

The sunlight shone into the living room through the banana trees in the front garden. Lawson sat with his coffee and reviewed his plans. With luck, he thought, there wouldn't be an autopsy, and even if there was well, they'd be expecting to find rum in his system—though not that much.

"So," his daughter Dorothea had said when he'd told her during one of their phone conversations that he'd adopted the habit of having two nips of rum with Coca-Cola every evening, "you're on the rum now, are you, Dad? Hope you don't get on to it like Grandpa Doyle used to!"

They had laughed at that, although Grandpa Doyle's rum drinking had not been a laughing matter. As Lawson could testify.

"Sometimes, Thea," he pretended to confess during that particular phone conversation, "I even have three! It seems to help my arthritis, you know."

By this ploy Charles Lawson hoped to escape detection as a suicide. Suicides always cast such gloom over funerals, and he wanted an elegant one. Besides, the mourners, what mourners there might be, would think he'd been depressed. "Poor Charles, I didn't know he was depressed—did you?"

Lawson didn't feel at all depressed. Seven years out of jail, he was happy with his life the way it was, and with the small triumphs of his day: getting the garbage out unaided, managing the back steps, walking on the nearby beach every second day.

Angela's death excluded, things had been good. Until that visit to the eye specialist.

Macular degeneration, she'd called it. Irreversible. With the cold logic of surgeons she had explained the progression of the disease and the likely time remaining to him before he was totally blind.

If only she hadn't used that word *totally,* Lawson thought, he couldn't adjust to *totally.* And what then? Would he have to go to Perth and live in a granny flat in his daughter's backyard like what's-his-name in *Scent of a Woman?* Blind at seventy-nine when you were too old to adjust?

Ah, no.

He could hear his daughter's voice: "Well, he always liked to have a rum and Coke in the evenings, officer, while he cooked dinner. Sometimes, I know he had two. But I don't think that would . . ."

"Mrs Williams, I'm sorry for your loss." He'd be firm, the constable. "You say, though, that he was in the habit of walking a little in the evenings after dinner—and sometimes swimming."

"Yes, yes, but I still don't see . . ."

"With respect, Mrs Williams, your father was an elderly man, and the beach there is famous for its rips."

It would work. Lawson was certain it would work. And he'd be sensible. No rocks in the pockets, he thought, no dumb shit like that.

He inspected the refrigerator. In the name of The Accident Theory, it was crammed with the usual fortnight's shopping he'd done two days ago, plus the things he planned to indulge in today. In the cupboard under the sink stood two bottles of rum, bought in different shops. The first bottle he took two nips from every evening, as usual. The second, ah, the second was for tonight.

For his last day Lawson had planned some special things, things that were Bad for You: a piece of pork for his last-ever dinner, some butter for his last breakfast toast, a block of dark chocolate to nibble on while he tidied the house, and bacon rashers for his breakfast. All these things were Bad For You, if you believed the nutrition books, and he had divested himself of them long ago.

Not today, he thought with relish as he broke out the bacon, placing half the rashers into a skillet, along with one egg.

He sniffed appreciatively as the unaccustomed smell of bacon wafted through the small apartment. God, how he'd missed bacon. Even in jail, they'd had it once a week. Still, his self-imposed regime had kept him healthy these seven years, if one didn't count the eyesight.

"I'm still standing," he sang. "Yeah yeah yeah."

He dropped two slices of bread into the toaster and had them done and buttered—ah, butter!—just as the bacon and eggs were ready.

Lawson was almost trembling with excitement as he sat down at the kitchen table to this breakfast. He'd brought in his daily newspaper, but he did not read with his magnifying glass as he usually did over his muesli and skim milk, but sat there, savouring every mouthful.

"This is the life, isn't it, Cynthia?" he told the old cat lying on yesterday's newspaper at the other end of the table.

The old cat raised her head and seemed to smile. She was a rescue cat, at least five years old when she'd arrived; Lawson had never been sure of her age. Both he and his wife had loved cats and they'd passed that love on to their only daughter. The cats would be okay after he was gone; Thea would fly them over to Perth. The old cat might pine a little, but the young cat, well, he'd go happily to anyone. Cats were never the same when you got them at six or seven weeks, Lawson thought to himself. For real devotion, you needed to have your cat born in the house.

At precisely 9 a.m. the phone rang. Thea rang every morning at this time from Perth. Lawson would've been happy if his daughter had rung him twice, or even once, a week, but he understood that it was Dorothea's way of accommodating the guilt she felt at having taken a job so far away.

Sometimes Charles Lawson couldn't figure out time. Sometimes it seemed only yesterday that Thea had been a toddler in nappies, smelling of Johnson's baby powder and peanut paste. How could she be a woman of forty?

After he'd hung up, Lawson ate some chocolate and studied the photographs on the sideboard. There was his wedding photo, taken in 1943—just twenty, he'd been on leave from the war in the Pacific for three days. His wife had worn a tailored suit with shoulder pads, a white silk blouse and a hat with artificial cherries. Later, they'd gone to Lennon's Hotel and danced to their song: a torch song called "Stella by Starlight".

Lawson sighed. When he'd first formulated his plan, he'd actually prayed to the spirit of his dead wife for guidance, for just the smallest sign. But who knew what was happening on the other side. If anything.

Lawson's eyes roamed on to the photograph of his youngest child James, looking macho in his Vietnam dress uniform. He passed on quickly to the photo of Thea on her wedding day. Lastly, there was his grandson Rocky, handsome in his cap and gown.

Lawson had plans for Rocky to deliver the eulogy. "He died as he lived!" Lawson could hear him saying, his fine voice ringing through the church—he intended to have a church service, with lots of flowers to brighten the occasion. No crematorium for him. Look at what had happened in America last year, or was it the year before? All those bodies, just lying around, and there was everyone thinking they'd been nicely cremated.

Charles Lawson felt a frisson of excitement as he reviewed his plans. Hell, he felt more alive than he had in years.

At 2 p.m. he placed his piece of pork in the oven. Since he intended to eat before he went to the beach, he needed to put the pork on now. The vegetables he could do later.

He lay down on his bed to read. He read every afternoon from two 'til four. It was one of the great pleasures of his life and had turned out to be a saving grace in jail. Sometimes he fell asleep over the book, but he was always up again at four to shower and watch *The Bold and the Beautiful*. He didn't care for the story lines, but he liked the clothes. He'd always had a fondness for stylish clothes, even more so now that he couldn't afford them.

Today he woke at five past four to the delicious smell of roasting pork. Lawson hadn't had pork in years. Too fatty, all the books said, and one, a book on Chinese medicine, which he'd taken out of the shire library searching in vain for a cure for his eyesight, had said that pork was "dampening to the spleen".

Well, Lawson thought, it didn't matter any more if he dampened his spleen. He made a pot of tea, ate some more chocolate and put on the vegetables. At 5 p.m. he set about getting the cats in for their dinner. The old cat was already waiting, but the young cat was uncharacteristically absent. Tonight he would lock them in the house as usual with a kitty litter tray in the bathroom.

He took the kitchen tidy bag and the compost bucket, and went carefully into the back garden, holding on to the wooden railing as he negotiated the four steps. When he returned to the kitchen after watering the garden, he found that the old cat had finished her first pass at the food and was washing her whiskers, while the young cat was still nowhere in sight.

Lawson had planned to eat at 6 p.m. before he went to the beach. With the young cat missing and his plan in jeopardy, he had no appetite. He removed the cooked pork from the oven and placed it on a rack to cool. He removed the vegetables and put them into a lidded vegetable dish. And all the while, he kept shuffling to the back door and beating on the empty cat food tin with a spoon, calling, "Bruiser! Yoohoo, Bruiser!"

Damn that cat. He was going to ruin all Lawson's plans.

Six o'clock came and went, and so did seven. Lawson wouldn't leave without having both cats locked in. He wanted to know—later on, when it mattered—that both his cats were safe.

He watched television abstractedly and called from the back door every half-hour, but the young cat did not return. By 9 p.m. Lawson was desperately worried. That cat was such a glutton; he'd never missed a meal in his life—what if he'd been knocked over? Lawson took the torch with its brand-new batteries and went out to search for him. He walked along the side of the road for a block in every direction, calling and shining the torch beam under bushes and along the grassy verges of the roads.

There was no sign of Bruiser.

Lawson returned to the house. He ate a boiled egg and a piece of bread and butter as he fitfully watched a '50s film on TV. The film was set in Africa in the 1890s. Some foolish female had gone there wearing corsets and stays and a long silk dress. Now she was having a terrible time of it.

Lawson left the lady to her fate at 10 p.m. She'd had to cut her waist-length hair. It was now curling perfectly around her face in the latest London style. Soon, Lawson knew, the woman would wrench her ankle and have to be carried by the hero. Who despised her.

Lawson called for Bruiser one more time. Then he jammed the sliding door ajar for the cat and went to bed. He was still concerned about him; nevertheless, he remained philosophical about The Plan.

There were plenty of other moonless nights.

Next morning, Lawson rose at dawn and dressed his small, spare figure, intending to go out and search for Bruiser again on the roadsides. But when he walked into the kitchen, the cat was there, clamouring for his breakfast as if nothing untoward had happened.

Charles Lawson experienced a stab of relief so intense it felt like pain. He sat down on the couch, and the cat sprang into his arms.

"Oh," he said, "you are *bad.* You upset all my plans!"

The cat purred his whipped-cream purr and snuggled his nose under Lawson's arm. Lawson stroked his plush tabby coat with its perfect stripes.

Tonight, he told himself.

He ate the rest of the bacon and eggs for breakfast. He was about to make a second cup of coffee, it was so delicious with cream and sugar, when Jennifer arrived.

"Good morning, dear, would you like a cup of coffee?" Lawson asked. He'd completely forgotten that he'd asked Jennifer to call in this morning so there would be someone to feed the cats and alert the police to the fact that he was missing.

Jennifer was tall and fair, with an athlete's body and

long, honey-coloured hair. She was the single parent of a girl of three from an unsuccessful marriage. She was divorced, quick to laughter, quick to tears.

This morning, she was very close to tears.

"How could she?" The young woman gulped at the coffee Lawson had placed before her. "How could she let me down at the last minute like that?"

Oh oh, Lawson thought. The P & C ball was something Jennifer had looked forward to for months. She'd intended to make an occasion of it, staying overnight with a girlfriend and returning in the morning—she'd even made herself a new dress.

Now her babysitter had let her down.

Lawson knew that he ought to offer to babysit, but he didn't want to mess up The Plan a second time. He pushed the box of tissues across the coffee table until it was in front of Jennifer.

"Never mind, dear," he said.

Jennifer cried through five tissues before Lawson spoke again.

"I'll do it for you," he said.

"Oh no. You can't," Jennifer sobbed. "Oh really, I never meant . . ."

Lawson was gently adamant. What was one more night, really?

"Bring Charlotte over at five. You'll have to show me how to use the microwave Thea gave me last Christmas, so I can reheat the baked dinner. Does Charlotte eat pork?"

"I don't know," Jennifer sniffled. "Probably."

Charlotte definitely ate pork. She also ate ice cream, Lawson discovered when they went to the beach before dinner—and chocolate pudding with whipped cream, which they had for dessert while they watched *The Lion King*, a video Jennifer had rented especially.

That night, as Lawson fell asleep to the sound of the sea and the old cat's snoring and Charlotte's gentle breathing in the cot beside his bed, he felt at peace with the world.

He'd forgotten how entertaining little girls were. He was so entranced with the child that, when Jennifer returned next morning, he thought he would offer to babysit again.

Then he remembered The Plan.

"Will you call in again tomorrow for coffee, dear?" he asked, trying to get everything back on track. "Around ten would be nice. The key's in a freezer bag in the geranium pot—in case I'm in the backyard and don't hear you."

There, Lawson thought as Jennifer drove off with a waving Charlotte strapped into her child seat. No one intending to commit suicide would ask someone to coffee next day. Thea would never know.

He spent a lot of time that day reliving the night before with Charlotte. He had a fierce longing that surprised him to do it all again—the ice creams, the beach, the swim in the shallows, the baked dinner with lots of gravy. Still, he didn't want to be a burden to Thea, and *totally* blind was too much.

The evening promised to be fine, with no storms or squalls. At 5 p.m. Lawson locked the cats in. At 5.30 p.m. he sliced some of the remaining pork, made sandwiches on wholemeal bread and wrapped them in greaseproof paper. Then he poured the new bottle of rum into an empty, one-and-a-half litre plastic bottle and filled it to the brim with Coca-Cola.

The frothing bubbles reminded him of the craze there'd been one year in his small bush school for friendship books, and how his best friend May had written in his:

> *Life is mostly froth and bubble.*
> *Two things stand like stone.*
> *Kindness in another's trouble.*
> *Courage in your own.*

Lawson felt a small surge of anxiety at the memory. Was he being cowardly? He didn't think so. Hadn't he been courageous long enough, never breaking down when they'd brought him the news of his son's death, nursing his wife through her terminal illness after he'd gotten out of jail?

He packed the rum and Coke and the sandwiches, along with a plastic cup, some paper serviettes and the empty rum bottle into his calico beach bag, put his swimmers on under his slacks and shirt and added two rolled-up towels and a cardigan. He said a last farewell to the cats, and made his way towards the beach just on sunset, hiding the front door key where Jennifer would find it in the morning.

He walked the four hundred metres slowly, keeping to the side of the road. A boy and a girl—high schoolers, probably—passed him, coming back from the beach, their arms around one another's waists. The girl was beautiful in a two-piece swimsuit that showed off her tan. The boy's fair hair shone in the sunlight.

Lawson wiped his fingerprints off the empty rum bottle and dropped it into a wheelie bin near the entrance to the beach. Then he made his way on to the dunes. To left and right, the shoreline stretched unbroken, unbuilt upon as far as the eye could see. The water glittered in the dying rays of the sun, and the sea air was wonderfully cool after the heat of the day.

He settled down in the dunes, spreading a towel to sit upon and unpacking his pork sandwiches. The new moon was low in the western sky. The beach still sported some people—a few late bathers, a gaggle of board riders, three fishermen and a number of people walking their dogs.

Lawson poured his first glass of rum and Coke and settled down to wait. He'd brought two plastic cups, he discovered, stuck tightly together. Still, that wasn't important.

The last light faded. To the south, the Byron Bay lighthouse began to flash. The swimmers left the water and the board riders came in, tramping up the sandy track that led through the banksias to the road.

Night fell. The fishermen began to use torches. A container ship appeared out at sea, travelling north. One by one, the dog walkers straggled in, and no new walkers appeared. An hour later, first one and then another of the fishermen began to pack up his gear.

Charles Lawson congratulated himself on picking the right night. A full moon night would've been hopeless, he knew. In this area, a whole night life came out when the moon was full. They sat around their illegal fires, playing guitars, drumming and smoking dope. The beach at new moon was different. The tribe tended to remain at home.

Lawson ate a couple of sandwiches and poured himself another plastic cup of rum and Coke by torchlight, hiding the light of the torch under the other towel he'd brought with him for just that purpose—best not to draw attention to himself or someone might be there at the coroner's enquiry: "I saw him in the dunes late that night. I thought it was unusual for him."

Careful, Charles, careful.

It was strange, he reflected, how he'd gotten used to the taste of rum and Coke. Scotch had been his drink in the good old days. Single malt. After jail, hardly anything. Until three months ago when he'd first come up with The Plan, he had never tasted rum, rarely tasted Coke. Now he enjoyed his two drinks every night.

Sitting there on the dunes, facing out to sea, he was relieved to find he felt none of the anguish he'd feared might overcome him at this point. He still wished for a sign; but never mind, he thought, toasting the new moon as it sank below the banksia trees to the west. Sign or no sign, his mind was made up.

At 9 p.m. the last fisherman stowed his gear and walked up through the dunes north of where Lawson was sitting, shining a torch to light his way on the track. For a second the arc of his torchlight swung wildly as he struggled to balance his gear.

That was when Lawson saw it: the shadow of someone else sitting in the dunes about sixty paces to the north of him. In that moment, whoever it was had been disturbed, and Lawson saw the red-hot-poker glimmer of a cigarette before the person cupped it again.

Charles Lawson felt a surge of annoyance. Who in their right minds came to the beach on a pitch-black night like this? Maybe it was some off-his-face hippy expecting a full moon. Well, he'd soon realise his mistake.

Lawson composed himself. The starlight was bright enough for him to see the stranger if he rose to his feet to leave. In that instant, he would be outlined against the sky. That should be enough to let Lawson know when he left the dunes.

Lawson ate one more sandwich and wrapped up the rest, keeping his eyes northward. The bottle was half-full. Did he really need to drink the rest? But the stranger was still there. Lawson took another sip.

What woke me? That is always a good question. Lawson pulled his cardigan tighter around his shoulders and listened. The moon was gone from the western sky. He could see the lights of a new container ship, far to the north on the horizon.

Listen.

It was the unbeautiful sound of a woman crying that had woken him. The sobs came from the shadow further along the dunes. They came softly on the north-easterly breeze, presenting Lawson with yet another moral dilemma. What was the correct course of action in this day and age when a woman was crying?

Charles Lawson sat tight. Ah, but it was hard to listen to, that soft, broken-hearted keening. Had the girl lost a lover, lost a spouse, lost a son? What was it that was causing her such grief?

Lawson held his left arm under the brown towel. He turned on the torch and checked his watch. Ten p.m. Go to it, girl, he thought. Get it out of your system, and then go home and have a nice sleep.

Half an hour later, the crying remained unabated. Lawson rose unsteadily to his feet and made his way over the sand dunes towards the stranger.

The crying stopped. "Who's there?" called a small voice.

"It's only me, dear," Lawson called as he walked by torchlight along the top of the dunes. "I thought you might like a little company. Would you like a drink or a pork sandwich?"

Lawson sat down on the dune beside the strange woman, poured her a rum and Coke and passed her a sandwich. By the light of the torch, which he no longer tried to conceal, he had a glimpse of shoulder-length hair and a gamine face. The rest of the woman was shrouded in shadow.

She gulped at the drink. "I needed that."

Lawson passed her a paper serviette. "Are you from round here?" he asked.

The strange woman shook her head as she lit a cigarette. In the light of the match flare, Lawson could see that her dark hair was done in a myriad small plaits. Dreadlocks? Lawson wondered, or were dreadlocks something else?

"I caught the last bus from Mullumbimby," she said.

"Oh yes?" Lawson ventured.

The woman made a gesture Lawson couldn't interpret. "I was desperate. I've been sitting on the dunes ever since. I forgot how cool it can get on the beach at night." She shivered.

Lawson produced his second towel, the one he'd brought to cover his torchlight, and placed it around the young woman's shoulders.

"How did you intend to get home?"

The woman shook her head. She held out her plastic glass for another drink. "Would you mind?"

Spurred on by the moment, Lawson managed to prise the two stuck-together cups apart, and poured drinks for both of them. They clinked plastic.

"Cheers!"

"Have you got a home to go back to?" Lawson asked, emboldened by this cameraderie.

"I s'pose I have. Back in Mullumbimby."

"And it seemed like a good idea to . . ." Lawson waved a hand towards the sea, now roaring at the base of the dunes below them.

The woman pulled the towel tighter around her shoulders. "What's it to you?"

"Surely there's some other alternative . . ." Lawson said, as much to himself as to the stranger.

Silence.

Lawson persisted. "How does your husband feel? If you don't mind my asking."

The woman's laugh was bitter. "Wayne? Oh, he's all right, he comes from here. He spends most of his spare time drinking with his mates."

Lawson stiffened. It couldn't be. "Wayne Abrahams?" he asked. Wayne, his main dealer from the old days.

The woman nodded. "But that's not the real problem." She pulled the scarf from around her throat. Even in the starlight Lawson could see the bruises.

Lawson wondered if he still had enough favours owing him to have Wayne taken care of. Probably not.

"How old are you—twenty-two, twenty-three?"

"I'm forty-four," the woman said with as much hauteur

as she could muster. "And what are you doing out here yourself at this hour, anyway?"

"It's my son's anniversary," Lawson lied. "He was killed in Vietnam some thirty years ago." That part at least was true.

"I'm sorry."

Lawson gazed out at the ocean as he considered the situation. The container ship was gone. The prawn fleet had crossed the bar. Their deck lights bobbed about as the boats changed position.

Give me a sign, Angela, give me a sign.

Nothing.

Lawson came to a decision. There were plenty of other moonless nights.

"Would you like to come back to my place with me? There are no buses 'til tomorrow and you can't stay here all night."

The woman began to gather up her things: a bag, a towel—hardly anything really, Lawson thought to himself. The girl didn't understand that planning was the first requisite for a successful suicide.

"I suppose I could ring Wayne," she was saying. "Maybe he'd come and get me. If he's not too drunk."

"Oh dear," Lawson said, "my phone's not working, and someone's vandalised the public phone near the shop. Wayne's not likely to go to the police about you, is he?"

The woman shook her head. "Lord, no!"

They began to walk slowly by the light of Lawson's torch towards the nearest entrance to the dunes. Now that Lawson was standing, he could see, dotted here and there along the beach, the glow of a cigarette, the glimmer of a small, illegal fire. Would his attempt have been successful, or merely a huge embarrassment?

A person would have to pick a rainy night, he thought to himself. But the prospect of the beach in driving rain didn't appeal at all.

"What's your name?" Lawson asked to make conversation as they walked along the dunes.

The woman glanced at him. He could just make out her face in the starlight. "Stella," she said. "But I don't like that name. Call me Star."

Lawson's heart stood still. Suddenly the universe blazed with possibilities. Who knew what was out there. *Who knew?* Somehow he'd find the courage to go on.

They came down the track from the beach to the road, Star supporting Lawson under one elbow when the track turned slippery. Already he was planning how he might persuade her to leave Wayne.

"I've got more rum back at my place," he said, lively now. "We can have ice in our drinks. Are you still hungry? I've got more left-over pork and roast vegetables."

8
A Dark Place

2002

You don't hear the thud when your head hits the door frame. You feel it. When he puts his hands around your throat, you don't hear the sounds you make as you struggle for air.

Later, examining your face in the bathroom mirror, praying there won't be something that you can't disguise with make-up, you don't feel anything much. Just apathy.

You're walled into apathy like someone in a tomb.

When people come to the front door, you don't answer when they knock. You hide.

When you go shopping, sometimes you have to wear a scarf and dark glasses. And long sleeves.

When your best friend tries the front door and you don't answer, she knows to come around the back. You're hiding under the kitchen table, waiting for whoever it is to go away.

"Christ, Star!" she says when she sees you. "Why don't

you leave him?"

I don't answer her. There's no point. She's married to this dependable man who doesn't smoke or drink. We don't go to one another's places. The only thing we've got in common is the children; we'd never have been friends if the children hadn't linked up. Don't get me wrong, she's my best friend. It's just she doesn't understand, that's all.

She doesn't understand that I can't leave him. There's the kids. There's us—there still is an Us. And lots of times, especially afterwards, he's wonderful.

It's as if there's two of Wayne, tied together in one person. Take the whole package or don't take anything at all. I took the whole package; just like my mother.

Of course, you need a little help to get by. The time I ran out of tranquillisers and couldn't get any for a week, I didn't think I could stand it a minute longer. I felt angry when he hit me; I screamed and cried. Once I even fought back. That was terrible.

I had to drink twice as much that week to hold me. To get me through. Now I make sure I never run out of Valium. I just drink the amount of alcohol I usually drink and take the amount of prescription chemicals I need to keep the household on an even keel.

People don't understand. I went to this psychologist once. She talked about ego boundaries and self-esteem. She didn't talk about love. About the rush you feel when he picks you up off the floor and carries you into the bedroom. About feeling again the way you used to feel when you were in love at eighteen. With us it's still alive, that excitement. It's not just some faded memory like it is for most people.

But I don't like being afraid. I don't like not knowing

when it's going to happen or what might set him off. I don't like the pain either. I take a lot of Panadol. When I can get it, I use Panadeine Forte, though I try to keep that up my sleeve for the really bad times.

I don't like having to take all those painkillers; they make me sick in the stomach. But the alcohol in the evenings settles that down pretty well. Some evenings are good: the boys watch TV, we sit in the kitchen and drink while I make the dinner; then we eat in front of the VCR with the children. All of us together. We're a family.

Late that night in bed he says, "Do you love me, Stella?"

Oh, I do.

"Aren't I good to you?"

A lot of the time, he is. But, like I said, lately I've fallen into apathy.

I'm buried in apathy. Put some lilies on my tomb.

9
Transference

2000

All this time I'd kept up my karate. When I got my 6th dan, I moved to Brisbane, intending to start a *dojo* up there. Life was heading in a new direction. I could make a living in a real profession: teaching. At first, Az refused to join me, but after six months the farmhouse we'd been renting all this time was sold, and she moved up, too. But bringing Az back to a big city was a huge mistake. She returned to the H. We started fighting again. And soon after that she met Hugh.

I fell apart when she left me. Couldn't eat, couldn't sleep. My teaching deteriorated. Eventually I decided, much against my will, that I needed help.

So I make the appointment.

It's late when I get there, and any fool could tell you I don't like the idea. I stand in the parking lot and look up at the building. It's tall and glossy and glamorous in the inner-city dusk. The sun is setting, and the windows on the west glitter like mirrors. Very pretty, if you like that kind of thing.

I push through the glass revolving doors into the foyer, tramp through the vestibule in my old motorbike gear, punch the button and wait for the elevator. My muscles ache and my split lip hurts. If it wasn't for my lip, I wouldn't be here; but when you're so bone tired from lack of sleep that a student can spit your lip . . .

Did I hear the word *sleep?* I used to sleep like a log. But that was before Azure left me.

The elevator climbs to the twentieth floor and stops. I step out into the corridor. There's a brass plaque on the opposite door. It reads: **DR A. WEST M.D.**

I run one fingertip over the brass. Very shiny, very nice. If you like that kind of thing.

The waiting room is the jungle scene from somebody's movie. I beat a path through the palms and accost the secretary. She checks me out in her appointment book and waves me back to the jungle.

"Snakes?" I demand, waving at the undergrowth.

She smiles at me, all *haute couture* and silver jewellery, as if I've just asked her the time.

"I assure you, Mr O'Neill, we have no snakes."

I wrench a chair from under a giant tree fern and sit down grimly. Some intrepid person has been here before me and left behind some magazines. I flip through them aimlesssly, keeping one eye on the jungle.

What the hell am I doing here anyway? I feel ridiculous. Six months have gone by and I still can't look at another woman, still can't sleep properly at night, still fantasise about smashing Hugh's head in—I would've too, if he hadn't shot through to Perth the moment he made off with Azure. The bastard.

Azure, Azure, I am obsessed with Azure. But she's gone. That's my problem. I come back from my reverie. The door to Dr West's office is open, and Dr West is standing in the doorway.

The time to take off is now. And yet, I need to talk to someone. If I don't sleep properly soon, my rising career in the martial arts will be up the creek, down the drain, finito. Besides, it's too late now; she's seen me. There she is, gesturing to me through a gap in the foliage. I push aside my misgivings and wade through the carpet to her door. This is where my troubles really begin.

Dr West motions me into her office which, I'm relieved to see, is clear of undergrowth. We sit down in comfortable chairs on either side of her desk.

"Mr O'Neill?" she asks, checking the card that Silver Jewellery has passed through the ferns to her on our way in.

I finger my split lip and stare at her. She's the first woman I've actually *seen* in months. It must be the shock or something.

"Mr O'Neill?" she says again.

I'd been expecting some old git who looked like Freud. Dr West is tall and slender, with dark hair and dark eyes and skin so clear she looks like a schoolgirl.

She doesn't look like Sigmund Freud at all.

We shake hands. Her fingers are long and slim, and pleasant to the touch.

"I'm Dr West, Mr O'Neill. Adrianne West."

"Michael O'Neill," I say. I wonder where we're supposed

to go from here.

There is silence. Dr West runs one hand through her short straight hair and plays with the biro she holds in those long slim fingers.

"Heavy day?" I ask. I don't wish to appear troubled or in need of help in any way.

"You could say that," Dr West says. Her voice is long and soft and flowing as her dress, and lazy hazy like those days of summer. I think she's very beautiful, although it's hard to say exactly why. She isn't glamorous. The effect she creates seems to come from within.

"And what can I do for you, Mr O'Neill?"

"Ever have a problem with snakes?" I ask her.

Dr West leans back in her black leather chair and eyes me speculatively. She seems to be waiting for something.

"Your waiting room," I say. "All that jungle." I'm enjoying myself, teasing her, making her think I'm some kind of nut. But I don't want to push it too far.

Dr West relaxes visibly. She throws the biro down on the desk, tosses her thick hair forward and laughs. Her laugh is rich and warm, and suddenly I don't feel so bad any more. Suddenly I feel as if everything's going to be all right somehow.

And she hasn't said a single word you might describe as therapeutic.

Four months go by. I see Dr West every Tuesday morning at ten o'clock. After the first six weeks she adds me to her Friday evening encounter group. (I'll smash the first person who laughs at this bit: Yoo hoo! It's Mike O'Neill at an encounter group. Don't try it.) Strange thing is, I get to like it after a while. It gives me a chance to study Dr West's technique.

I've never met a woman who could produce such an effect, such a blending of warmth and distance—so different from the flame and fire of Azure. West is subtle. She's got what we call in karate "power in reserve", a kind of meekness-mildness that you know is anything but. I don't even know where she lives. No one does. Dr West is a very private person.

It occurs to me that I might recover more quickly if I read some books on psychology, understand the process, so to speak. Besides, I like the way Dr West smiles when I say something "relevant and meaningful" in group. If I study the books a bit on the side, I can be relevant and meaningful more often. So I get these books on psychology out of the library—nothing too heavy, you understand—and I begin to read them in the evenings.

I chop a load of firewood as the winter approaches, and every night after dinner I sit before the fire with my books, swotting up on points that might hold Adrianne's West's interest. Once, we get so meaningful we run on into Freddie the Manic's hour fifteen minutes, which is a kind of minor triumph for me. Dr West prides herself on her punctuality with the clients.

Reputations are funny things. Even though I'm forty-five, I've got the reputation of being a spunk—I guess with all that training now I *look* like a spunk, even if I'm not. So on this particular Friday evening when Dr West locks eyes with me across the group (I always make sure I sit dead opposite her), I could almost swear she was coming on to me.

I lie in bed that night and think about it. Nah, it's not possible. And yet . . . is West married? If she is, why does she wear her wedding ring on the wrong finger? And why does she give off such a solitary air?

Even before this, I've developed the habit after group sessions of sitting on my bike under an overhanging Moreton Bay fig tree, waiting for her to come out of the building. She's always last. I tell myself I'm only there to make sure she gets safely to her car, but I don't know. My feelings are confused. I can't sort them out.

I care for her in some strange way I don't understand.

The night after all the heavy eye contact, I take off my wedding ring when I come home and drop it into the top drawer of the bureau where I keep my shirts. It leaves a white mark on my finger, for I am tanned from the hours of work I do on the road, and it's a long time before the mark fades away.

Of course I'm still in love with Azure, but lately I've begun to think less about her and more about Adrianne West. I even begin sleeping properly again at night.

No doubt about it: Dr West is one hell of a good therapist.

One Saturday morning the doorbell rings as I'm showering after my workout. I knot a towel around my waist and go to answer it.

Red fingernails. Tight jeans. Long, L A hooker-blonde hair.

It's Azure, suitcase and all, on the top step. For an instant I'm confused. Has she always worn her jeans that tight? Has she always been so . . . *unsubtle?*

"What happened to Hugh?" I ask.

Azure tosses her hair. Hell, has it always been that blonde?

"It's over. He's gone to Europe," she says.

Wasn't it just like Hugh to go to Europe? Hugh, of the *nouveau riche* accent, the Merc and the flab. I have a beautiful flash fantasy of him sinking slowly, p'raps somewhere in the Carribean.

"Aren't you going to invite me in?" Azure's saying, running her nails along my shoulder and down my bare arm.

Unsubtle.

I let her in and, even before I do, I know what she's intending.

"Miss me?" she says huskily, fumbling at the knot in my towel. For some reason, I'm hanging on to it.

"Yes," I mutter. But an image of Dr West laughing at one of my clever psychological points distracts me, and Azure has to work a little harder to get what she wants.

By now she's got me backed up against the fireplace. The knot finally gives way, the towel slips to the floor and Azure flings herself upon me. I gather nothing much had been going down before Hugh went to Europe.

For one wild, crazy moment as I cling to the mantelpiece, I think of holding out. But bugger it, I can't. I let her drag me down on to the sofa. She begins to make love to me in earnest, and it's so good after all that pain to let go and feel nothing but pleasure. The pleasure seems to flow like a chemical in my blood, mounting higher with every move we make.

"I missed you," Azure keeps saying all though it. "Missed you . . . missed you . . ." In rhythm to my strokes.

"I—missed—you—*too!*" I gasp. But even as I come I'm thinking of Dr West.

It's hours later when Azure drives away, blonde hair flying in the wind. I come back inside and sit down thoughtfully on the remains of the sofa. It's then I realise: I am as good as hung.

Bit by bit, I've fallen in love with Dr West.

The following Friday night when her car pulls out of the parking lot, I follow her. It's not far—ridiculously close, in fact, when I think of all the ways I tried to get the her address. Turns out it's a little Edwardian cottage in Spring Hill, perfectly restored, with a wrought iron verandah on the front, brick fireplace, the lot.

I park at the bottom of the hill and walk by after she's gone inside. I'm jubilant. I know where she lives.

And what good does that do me? I think as I'm riding home and the cold air hits me. Knowing where she lives doesn't really tell me what I want to know.

I stop at a red light on the corner of Leichhardt and Albert Streets. On my right there's a chemist shop. Next door is a hardware store with a sign flashing:

KEYS CUT HERE

KEYS CUT HERE

Of course. If I had a key to her cottage I could go there one Friday night while she was at group. Just once, so I would know if there was somebody else. I wrestle with my conscience all the way home. In the end I do exactly what I had intended to do all along.

I'm not going to tell you how I got that key to copy, though I kind of enjoyed all the cloak-and-dagger stuff; it was just like being back in the bureau. But no one should ever have the key to somebody else's place, not like that. Of course it was okay for me, I'm not a dangerous person—but some people? Well, it's hard to tell.

After I go through the house the first time, I never intend to go back. Why should I? I've found out what I need to know: she lives alone. And I don't take a single thing. Not a hairpin, not a scarf. Nothing.

I keep the key I had made. But that's just sentimentality, I guess.

At this stage things are not yet out of hand. Azure keeps coming around. She wants to move in with me, but I won't let her in case Dr West rings and Azure answers the phone. Not that West ever does ring. She makes a point of not mixing with the clients after hours. She calls it "keeping a therapeutic distance". But all things considered, it's not a bad time. I've still got everything under control, even though I'm fantasising non-stop about Dr West and making love to Azure 'til I'm exhausted.

While we make love I fantasise I'm taking the good doctor to dinner. She's wearing cream silk—everything she has on is cream silk, right down to her underwear, all edged with lace. Azure is amazed at my stamina; but all I've got to do is think of Dr West in cream underwear.

The rest is a cinch.

Every Friday night the group meets for drinks afterwards in a little restaurant and bar called The Windmill. I've never been a big drinker, the price when you're training next day is too high, but I like the company. It makes a nice change from my torrid nights with Azure, and I look forward to it, even though Adrianne doesn't go.

This night the group's main focus of discussion is Dr West's suggestion that we consider having our eggs or sperm frozen to safeguard our genetic inheritance, in case we never marry. At first I dismiss the idea as barmy. But when West confides that she's going to do it and names the clinic she intends to go to, I think, wot-the-hell, maybe I'll bump into her there—wouldn't that be romantic.

Freddie is late for our drinks at The Windmill, which isn't unusual. He's always late for everything except his appointments with Adrianne West. When he finally does arrive, he's wildly excited. He rushes up to us at the bar and begins in his manic way.

"Anyone want to see Dr West's husband? This is *it,* people, the chance of a lifetime! See your therapist's private life! I was just driving by, *pure accident,* and I saw them having dinner in this place on Coronation Drive. Isn't astrology *grand?* My stars told me something amazing would happen today!"

"How do you know it's her husband?" I ask sourly. I feel like knocking him down, giving him enough stars to amaze him for the rest of his life.

"Well, maybe it's not her husband," says Freddie, master

of the Hiroshima effect, "but whoever it is, it's pretty clear what's going down. And you should see this guy! He's blond. Like you," he turns to me, "only better looking. He's about six-foot-two, and he's—"

There's a theory in psychology that manics don't live very long. I can see why. I signal to the barman for a double Scotch—make it a triple, better still, an octagonal—and I leave after fifteen minutes, pleading a tournament in the morning.

Out on the street the rain is falling as I pad the three ks to the restaurant Freddie has named, and all the while there's this strange sick feeling in my stomach.

It's a good restaurant: soft lights, lace curtains, shine of polished wood, glow of silver. Adrianne is sitting at a table near the window, and the man Freddie described is with her.

She's wearing cream silk.

I stand across the street with my back to the river and watch them until I can't bear the feeling any more, then I walk back to my bike in the rain. I take the worst possible route, hoping a gang of punks or some skinheads might pick me, but my anger goes before me like a cloud that people sense, and everyone I see on that walk avoids me. Some even cross the street.

The next few weeks are indescribable. I catch the flu and lie in bed moaning while Azure makes vats and vats of soup. When anyone from the group rings up, I croak into the phone pleading illness and insanity, God knows it's the truth.

When I'm well, Freddie comes round and tries to reason with me. "*Think* of your personal growth!" he cries. But I won't go back.

Dr West maintains her therapeutic distance; she doesn't even telephone. I could be dead for all she cares, I think. But I know, deep down, I'm not angry with her. I'm angry with me.

I go back to her house one more time and go through it in a cold fury. The guy's moved in all right, good and proper, and if I don't change the subject soon, I think I'll throw up.

There's a tournament on in Sydney in six weeks time, a tough one for which I am not prepared. I fill out the entry form and send it off with the entry fee. Then I put away the books on psychology and take my workouts up to four hours a day, six days out of seven.

Twice a week I ride to the home of my old master Mr Chun Tie and train with him in his garden resplendent with bougainvillea and bamboo. And afterwards, over fragile cups of China tea we plan our strategy and refine my technique.

Only once do I mention Adrianne West and, when I do, Mr Tie remarks in his strange high voice, "She is wise?"

I nod with veiled eyes, pushing away fantasies of cream underwear.

"But," Mr Tie glances hard at me for an instant, and I hope he can't read my mind, "she is married."

That's all he says. I wonder if I'll ever be even half the master he is. I try; but maybe I'm still too young or something. Wisdom always seems to elude me.

I've never liked tournaments. I guess that must sound

funny coming from someone with a 6th dan, but I don't like to fight. Still, I'm accustomed to these feelings and I have learnt to handle them. To have a reputation is necessary for my new livelihood.

I fight my way through to the finals until, just as Mr Tie had predicted, only Yukio Mishimoto stands between me and the championship. Mishimoto is good, but in the end my training shows and I beat him. I get my picture on the front cover of *Martial Arts in Australia,* my face covered in blood and three ribs broken, executing a flying kick I can't believe I've done.

Strange how victory affects some people. I can take being beaten almost to a pulp—but winning? I never did know how to handle it.

Aching to see West one more time, I dig out the note I'd made of the clinic where West said she intended to go to preserve her DNA. I hijack Az into coming along with me as cover, but I'm out of luck: West isn't there when we are. The future might have my DNA, but my real reason for going, my million-to-one chance of seeing West, fails.

I fall back on the one thing I know that won't let me down: work. I get on with my life. I still think a lot about Adrianne West but I'm stuck with the facts. She's married and I'm obsessed.

Spring comes. The trees lining the road to my *dojo* burst into bloom. I take to sitting outside on the verandah by myself after dinner, watching the fruit bats in the mango tree, and doing long rides on my bike in the night like a drug runner. But no matter where I go—Redcliffe,

Stradbroke, Noosa—I always end up back in Spring Hill.

Standing in the shadows, fingering the key in my coat.

Things get worse and worse with Azure. One weekend I demolish the garage with a sledgehammer, a trick I learned from an old kickboxer who had a rocky relationship with his wife. But even that doesn't help me much, and I know she'll have to go. Funny, the kickboxer's been married thirty-two years. It worked for him; but it sure as hell didn't worked for me.

I begin to think more and more about seeing Adrianne again—maybe just at a distance. After all, I reason, what harm could that possibly do? Besides, it might help me to put things in perspective.

Putting things in perspective . . . I torture myself with this idea for weeks, and one particularly beautiful Friday afternoon I crack. I come in from the back garden where I've been building a rock wall to try to work off my confusion. I take a shower, pull on an old track suit, do a few stretching exercises and begin to run.

Azure twigs at the last moment that something is up. She comes down to the gate and begins screaming.

"Where are you going, you bastard! Come back!" And things of a similar ilk. But I don't turn round.

The sun is setting behind the mountain. The trees look like black lace against the sky. I run steadily, keeping an even pace, and gradually Azure's screams fade in the distance.

Still, I feel wistful. Black lace . . . Azure has always worn black lace underwear. I loved it once. Now it seems—there's that word again—*unsubtle.*

I run on in the grip of my obsession. Night falls. The

streetlights come on. It's eight o'clock by the time I get to Spring Hill. I go first to Adrianne's cottage—habit, I guess—but the lock's been changed. Hah, I always knew she'd never last with him.

I'm in a kind of euphoria as I walk to the building where she works. I sit down under a jacaranda tree in the park across the road and try to arrange my feelings. The first stars are coming out, the new moon is sinking, and I don't have a hope in hell of arranging anything. Least of all, my feelings.

After an hour the high I'm on begins to dwindle; I even consider going home. Just then I see Freddie come out of the foyer of Dr West's high-rise, followed by the rest of the group in dribs and drabs. They disperse to their cars and drive off towards The Windmill.

Now the street is empty. I wait for Adrianne to appear, but she doesn't come. Black fantasies run amok in my head. Is she dead? Abducted by terrorists? I never read the papers or watch TV.

I tear across the road, lope through the foyer and fling myself into the elevator. On the way to the twentieth floor, reason comes to my aid: Adrianne's okay; just heartbroken over my leaving. She stays back on Friday nights in the hope I might come to her. Ah Adrianne, if only I'd cracked sooner. All this pain we've suffered could've been avoided.

The carpet is soft under my feet as I push through the waiting room jungle. Now I'm almost at the doorway of her office.

"Heavy day?" I'll say.

Adrianne will be sitting at her desk, eyes wet with tears, dark hair tangled. She'll give a little cry on seeing me. The magazine she's been sobbing over will slip to the floor, and there I'll be on the cover of *Martial Arts in Australia,* bloodstained, broken-ribbed, flying kick and all.

I'll dash to her side. She'll tell me the man in the restaurant was her brother who's just back from New Guinea, the New Hebrides—New Anywhere. I'll grab her in my arms and kiss her . . .

My eyes mist at the thought.

When I come to, a strange woman dressed all in blue is watching me closely from behind Adrianne's desk. Her hair is long and thick and crimpy, the colour of ironbark honey.

"Can I help you?" she asks warily.

I hate reality. There's always someone kicking you in the teeth.

"Where's Dr West?" I manage to say.

"I'm sorry," the strange woman says, "but Dr West and her husband" (I wince at the word) "left for India two months ago. Perhaps I can help you," she adds gently.

I'm about to refuse, turn and go, but reason comes to my rescue. And the woman is still speaking.

"I'm Dr Bostock. Suzanne Bostock." Her voice seems to flow like water.

I nod and sit down. Thoughtfully. Of course she could never replace Dr West, but I need to talk to someone. My stints on the verandah are getting longer, my sleep is almost non-existent, and the garage is gone.

"I don't usually see clients at this hour, Mr . . .?"

"O'Neill," I venture. "Michael O'Neill."

"But as you were one of Dr West's clients, I'll make an exception for you."

She's riffling around in the files as she speaks, a tiny thing with slim ankles and blue high heels. Very different from Adrianne, and not at all like a schoolgirl.

"Ah." She finds my file. Now she crosses to the desk, sits and opens it in front of her.

I watch her as she reads. She's wearing amethyst earrings, and I can see her, actually *see* her.

"Hmm . . ." Dr Bostock leans back in the black leather chair. I check out her hands. There are no rings.

"It says here you suffer from obsession, Mr O'Neill."

I try my bashful look. "Well, sort of."

"Sort of," she says, and smiles.

It's a good joke. She and I both know there's no such animal as "sort of" in obsession. Suddenly I don't feel so bad any more. Suddenly I feel as if everything's going to be all right.

"Would you like to tell me about it?" Suzanne Bostock is saying.

I begin at the beginning. The day I first met Dr West.

10

While There's Life . . .

2005

On her way to the river for another attempt, Star decided to say goodbye to Ron; he'd been a good neighbour. They weren't in and out of one another's houses, nothing like that, but she knew he was there. On bad nights his lights were a comfort to her. She didn't intend to tell him what she had planned.

"Want a cup of coffee?" he asked.

She thought, the river will wait.

Ron made plunger coffee and opened a packet of Scotch Finger biscuits. "Where's the family?'

"Wayne's taken the boys camping for the weekend."

"Ah."

They sat there dunking. It was the first pleasant company Star had had in a long time. O'Neill and Azure had moved to Brisbane, Baby had fled to Sydney; she heard he'd married. Lawson had gone dotty, talking to his cats on and off. Some days were all right, but you could never tell. She hardly saw him any more.

Wayne had won. She was completely isolated.

"Life's funny," Ron said as they were on their second cup of coffee. "When the oncologist told me I had cancer, I was like, Whoooo! What are we going to do about it?"

Star paused with the coffee cup halfway to her lips. Ron had never mentioned cancer before.

"He looked very serious, the oncologist," Ron went on. "And I mean *very*. 'There's nothing we can do,' he said."

Ron tossed down another mouthful of black coffee. "I took a deep breath. It was starting to sink in. 'How much time have I got?' I asked.

"The oncologist hesitated. 'Well,' he said. 'In your case, maybe five months.'

"I don't remember the journey home," Ron continued. "The first thing I do remember is sitting on the sofa in the lounge room. The Kid was out, the clock said 4.00 p.m. Somewhere along the way, I'd lost three hours, and now, in five months or so, I was going to lose my life. Want another Scotch Finger?"

Star took another. Until that moment, she hadn't known how hungry she was.

"I poured myself a stiff bourbon and sat there," Ron said. "At first I was angry. Why me—what had I ever done that was so wrong? Hell, I even bought water, the spring water I made the coffee with just now—you get it too, don't you?"

Star nodded. It was comforting to know the river was still there. It would still be there when she needed it.

"The flat was *so* quiet." Ron passed her the packet of Scotch Fingers. "I just sat there and let the whole thing crash down on top of me, like a wave you take that goes wrong. I was going to die. Cripes, I can't begin to tell you how I felt. Then, after a while, something changed in me and I thought, Well, if that's how it is, that's how it is. Might as well accept it."

"Why didn't you tell me?"

Ron looked sheepish. "Well, you know. You've got enough on your plate. Anyway, there I sat in this totally quiet flat, resigning myself to the inevitable. The Kid was out raging somewhere—riding his trail bike around the nature reserve, ripping up the countryside. He was sixteen then, a hard kid to raise. The neighbours were always complaining about him, remember?"

"Yes." She remembered Wayne waving a rake at the teenager one day. Back in the good old days when she'd first got back with him.

"At 5 o'clock, I began planning my funeral. I'd just picked out the pallbearers when out of the blue, it hit me." Ron thumped himself on the chest. "IF I DIE, WHO'S GONNA LOOK AFTER THE KID?

"My ex, she'd remarried, and the new man and The Kid didn't get on. Well, I thought, the ex is out, even though she's his mother. Who else was there? I had no brothers, no sisters. My father was eighty-two; he couldn't do it. Besides, he'd remarried and his new wife didn't want him to have anything to do with us, apart from a card at Christmas. The Kid couldn't go there. What to do?

"And that's when I decided I couldn't die, after all. Just when I was getting used to the idea and thinking what music I'd like at the service. No one else was going to look after that kid. They'd toss him into foster care and he'd end up in jail. Can't let that happen, I thought. He might be a bastard, but he's my kid and he needs me.

"So I had another drink and pulled myself together. By the time I heard The Kid's bike coming down the road, I had the water on for the spaghetti and was frying up the mince for the sauce—he loves spaghetti bol, it's his favourite.

"And that's it, really." Ron spread out his hands. "All that was six years ago, the oncologist can't believe it! I swear I was ready to let them take me until I remembered The Kid. Funny how life works out, isn't it?"

He gave her a hug at the door. "Have a good one."

When Star reached the road, instead of turning right to the river, she turned left for home.

11

Who Said Cats Can't Talk

2005

The cats know the sounds of the approaching morning. The young cat starts stirring around dawn; galloping up and down the stairs, coming to the bedroom door and calling. She's hungry. All the dry cat food I put down for the night is gone. She's only nine months old and still growing.

But I know, and the old cat knows, that when I get up at 8 o'clock, there'll be clean plates, fresh cat food, fresh milk (powdered, alas) and freshly grated cheese. The old cat wouldn't eat cheese for a long time, but she loves it now.

At ten to eight, one of the buses bound for the high school goes past on the road east from me. You can hear the long haul of it picking up speed, changing up through the gears. I never want to get up in the mornings now that my sight is bad, but I've promised myself I won't stay in bed after eight. It's a bad feeling, lying there hearing everyone else going about their business. You feel like something washed up on a beach.

Flotsam, jetsam. Wrack. Ruin.

Even so, I lie there until the next bus trundles by at 5 past 8, then I speak to the old cat who's waiting patiently at the end of the bed.

"Okay, Cynthia, time to get up now."

The old cat—that's you, Cynthia, we're talking about you now—was a rescue cat Angela and I took in years and years ago. In a fit of whimsy my wife Angela named the small grey cat Lady Cynthia Asquith, claiming the cat had an expression similar to the English writer's in photographs. Time whittled this down to Cynthia. Now no one but I know the origins of the name, know that the old arthritic cat in No. 1 is really called Lady Cynthia Asquith.

I push back the covers and sit on the edge of the bed. I put on the long football socks I got at St Vinnies and a tracksuit from my daughter Thea's ballet period.

I avoid the mirror. I'm starting to see my father's face in mine, now that I'm old. He looks back at me, cowed by the grind of the dairy farm. Cowed by life.

I go and sit on the toilet. While I'm there the young cat comes in and lifts herself off the floor, front paws up to nudge at my hand with her nose. Her little part-Siamese, part-tortoiseshell face looks like a pansy. I couldn't afford another cat, but I took her in to save her life when she was abandoned under the flat next door.

You remember that, don't you, Cynthia? You remember how we got the young cat?

And the old cat talks to him. Lawson thinks it says:

Ah, Mr L, I well remember the night the young cat came to the door. It was summer, the day had been hot. It had rained the night before. There she stood on my doorstep.

"I was wondering," she began in a high voice, and I saw then that she was barely more than a kitten, "if you might have a vacancy. My mother has disappeared, and my brothers and sisters. And I'm thirsty."

"No vacancies," I said. Hard. "And there's plenty of water on the road." You can't take in every kitten that comes to your door. I had a standard of living to uphold.

"I was thinking more along the lines of milk." Hesitantly.

"Oh very well," I said, "you can have some milk, but then you must be on your way."

I showed her the bowl. She approached and began to drink without any pretense to good manners. I felt a stab of pity for her, even though I'd been a professional bush rat assassin until well past middle age and had a reputation for ruthlessness. I had never had kittens, preferring my career to the pursuit of toms.

"I suppose you'll be wanting something to eat as well," I said and pushed my dish of top-brand food for retired executive cats across the kitchen floor to her with my good foot.

The dish was almost full. Truth to tell, I hadn't cared much for food lately. Mr L had outdone himself, getting the most expensive cat food money could buy in a supermarket. Still, I didn't feel interested. The only thing that did take my fancy was cooked fish from the corner store with the batter removed, but Mr L couldn't afford that more than once or twice a year.

Watching the young cat, a catling, really, as my mother used to say, wolf down the food, I felt a sudden twinge of interest. It was all I could do to restrain myself from shouldering her away. In the end I decided she'd throw up if she ate any more, so I did push her away. And the food, when I tasted it, tasted better than it had in weeks. Months.

So you see, the accusations levelled at me that I took in this kitten, catling, because I had grown soft in my old age, are grossly untrue, mere fabrications concocted by my enemies to discredit me. I am still ruthless. It is an essential characteristic in an assassin, and one I have retained to this day.

The kitten did not speak to me any more that night, except to tell me that her name was Milo. Then she crawled into a basket of Mr L's pending mending and passed out. Mr L has had that basket for as long as I can remember, but very little of the mending pending ever gets done.

I sat in front of the TV and washed my face, paying careful attention to my whiskers, but the program on kangaroos did not interest me. The kitten had begun to snore.

Milo, I thought to myself, it's an impossible name, I can't live with it. Mr L can't be out in the dusk, calling, "Milo! Milo!" like a fool.

I thought for a long time and then I decided: we would call her Lady Ottoline Morrel. For those of you who aren't well read, Lady Ottoline was a great patron of the arts in England in the Edwardian era. She used to dye her hair purple and smoke marihuana, if I've read the veiled references in Sassoon's autobiography correctly.

Lady Ottoline Morrell it shall be, I decided. I'll let her know in the morning.

A new decade, a new century—a new millenium. Who would've thought, Cynthia, when I was just a boy of twelve in a cassia tree, hiding from the farm chores, reading poetry and wanting to die before I was forty, that I would get to see the year 2005? *I* never thought it. I would've had to imagine myself eighty-two, and that wasn't possible. I was never going to be that old. Oh no, not I. Not in that tree with its long spikes of yellow flowers hanging down, and my hair, thick as a thatch, upon my head.

I was in love with the war poets at that time—Wilfred Owen, Rupert Brooke, Sigfried Sassoon. I had a photo of Brooke in my room; he was all I wanted. I kept thinking on my long walks between the chores and the poetry that if he hadn't died I could've met him later and entranced him.

I knew, even then, I was gay. Turned out, I was—in spite of Angela, God rest her soul. In spite of the kids.

Byron Shire's an odd place to live, with its plethora of weirdos and "healers". There's always some new crazy coming along. Now some maniac around here thinks it's his public duty to go around terminating any cats he finds out after dark. He prowls the streets at night, looking for them. He even wrote a letter to the local paper about it; about how hard it was for him to do what he did, but how he had to, you know, to save the wildlife. He's not only a psychopath, he's a fool, but that's the way with zealots. Could this be why Bruiser disappeared? I'd hate to think so.

The food's the best that Mr L can afford. We eat Dine and the fish lines of Whiskas. We also eat Black & Gold tuna, but I don't want that to get about.

One big improvement in the daily fare: because I said yes to "the little homeless kitten", we had cheese added to our diets. Mr L did it for the kitten's sake, to add another little meal, but it is I who have benefited the most. Mornings when the Lady Ottoline is too busy chasing lizards to come in, I get to eat both bowls. This is not greed on my part, but merely commonsense. Grated cheese doesn't keep. Economy is what drives me as I force down that second bowl.

I look forward to that cheese every morning more than I can say. Sometimes, 'specially if it's raining, it's the only thing that gets me out of bed. The highlight of my day, you might say.

Talking of highlights, Cynthia, the highlight of my year when I was a kid was the Agricultural Show. Did you know we won Best Pig of Show one year? The old man was ecstatic. But winning or losing, I loved the show. It got me away from the farm for a while.

My mother was interested in the flowers, but all I ever wanted to see was sideshow alley. My father had an old family friend called Paddy Smith, a man who worked occasionally on the farm and who seemed to know everyone on the edge of the underworld. With him, I got into all the shows for free, while my mother inspected the fruit and the flower displays. She hated sideshow alley: Jimmy Sharman's Boxing Troupe, the Snake Pit and, best of all to me, the Lady Frozen in the Ice—there was a wonderful picture of the woman on the marquee, lying there in her bathing suit all glamorous like Lana Turner. Frozen in a gigantic block of ice.

Paddy knew the spruiker for the frozen lady. He let Paddy and me in between shows. The block of ice was all I had hoped for, set upon a trestle table, but much to my surprise, it was hollow.

The end had been prised off the block. The lady crawled out and sat on the edge of the table, saying, "For Christ's sake, Fred, give me a cigarette!" She was a peroxide blonde and didn't look nearly as beautiful as she did on the marquee. Still, I hung around while Paddy and the spruiker and the frozen lady, whose name was Gloria, smoked and chatted for about twenty minutes.

The spruiker pulled my ear playfully, but there was menace behind it. "You won't say anything to anyone about this, will you, kid?"

"Charlie's all right," Paddy said. "He likes secrets."

Ah yes, we had our secrets, Paddy and I . . .

When the twenty-minute break was up, the spruiker put a fresh towel into the block for Gloria to lie on, and she crawled back in. He lifted the square end of ice back on to the block, and set it in place with a blow torch. Then he opened the tent flap and another dozen or so people started filing in.

Gloria lay, eyes open, unblinking, one arm over her head as if the force of the glacier she was supposed to have been preserved by had flung her into that position.

The women said, "Oo, will you look at that—is she alive?"

"Suspended animation," the spruiker explained.

"Look at that bathing suit, the brazen hussy!"

"She can't help it, Mavis. She didn' know she was going t' be knocked down by a glacier that morning."

I hung around. I didn't want to leave. It was my first taste of show business.

On hot nights, Ottoline and I go out through the upstairs bedroom window and sit on the roof of the apartment next door. It's only one storey, not like ours. Sometimes Felix, the tom from across the road, climbs the lilli pilli tree and joins us—he's allowed to stay out all night.

The three of us sit on the ridge pole in the dew, inhaling the night air. It smells of salt, and frangipani in the summer. We watch the moon rising over the ocean and the stars wheeling through space.

The things you see when you're up there! Are they satellites, or UFOs? Personally, I don't know, don't care. But Felix has his theories.

It's a shame Mr L can't come out and sit on the ridge pole, too.

And a shame, Lady Cynthia, that retribution sometimes takes so long.

I'd gone into Brunswick Heads to submit my three-monthly rent review form. The government lets huge multinationals defraud them of tax worth millions, but God forbid they should overpay some pensioner by twenty cents a fortnight.

I stood in line while the queue behind me grew. Finally only one person was ahead of me, a very down-at-heel looking male, the sort whose eyes you avoid on the street, in case he asks for money. I stood well back and drifted away as the man who'd seen better days explained his predicament to the girl at Reception.

It seemed the down-at-heel one had been evicted from his flat for non-payment of rent. Now he was living in his car. His partner had died; he'd had a nervous breakdown, etc. etc. I was about to tune out from all this misery, when something about his voice stabbed at me. People can change a lot in forty-five years, change so much you can't recognise them. Voices are another matter. As the shabby man at the desk unrolled his story I was suddenly pulled back in time.

Could it be?

I shuffled much closer than was allowed, and listened. Old people can get away with murder, if they look suitably vague. It was him all right, my old downfall, Jamie Stanborough. No longer glamorous.

How are the mighty fallen and the weapons of war perished, as they say in the Bible. I got to read the Bible a lot in jail.

The girl on Reception had heard enough. She directed him up the road to St Vincent de Paul. I held my newspaper in front of my face and pretended to be reading about the day's atrocities as he passed me. Out on the street he turned up his collar against the southerly. I watched him walk slowly away.

And did I feel vindicated, Cynthia, did I feel triumphant to see brought low the person whose perfidy had caused me to give up academia?

Well, did you?

I didn't feel anything. It was all so long ago. As if the catastrophe that changed my life had happened to somebody else.

Water under the bridge.

Blood under the bridge, more like.

12

Last Train to Parthenia

2006

He found the amulet on a dark and drizzly night when the city seemed asleep on his way to work. His gang worked from midnight to dawn in the inner-city circle of StateRail, Sydney, walking the tracks trailing spot-welding gear to repair any cracks they found in the rails. Mostly they were underground, walking miles every shift to ensure the safety of those thousands of commuters who entrusted their lives every day to StateRail.

Occasionally they found strangers in the tunnels: sobbing girls with bottles of vodka, waiting for the first morning train to despatch them; truculent men with similar intentions.

"What happens to these people?" Johnson asked Colin, the head ganger, after he'd encountered his first would-be suicide.

"We take them back to the office, Bob. The manager

gives them a dressing-down."

"That's all?"

Colin placed a hand on Johnson's shoulder. "If they're really ratty, someone calls the mental health team."

How many people, Johnson wondered, used the railway to top themselves? StateRail didn't advertise, never seemed to put out any figures.

But work on the tracks of the inner-city circle suited him. With O'Neill gone to Brisbane, he'd returned to the city of his youth. Although he was ten years older than the rest of the gang, he had no trouble. Insomnia was just one of the many problems he'd suffered after Vietnam. He'd been walking miles at night for years.

The concentration needed for the job suited him, too. It was almost a meditation: eyes on the rails, lights from the gang's helmets flashing across the soot-encrusted walls of tunnels. Occasionally odd things happened that kept them on their toes—an unscheduled engine passing through, for instance. Although they carried 2-way radios to warn them of these trains, the reception didn't always work. The gang had to be ready to get the welder off the rails at a moment's notice and hurry to the safety of the alcoves if they were in a tunnel, or a safety hole if they were in the open.

The first time Johnson crouched in a safety hole with Colin, clinging to the safety rail, waiting for the train they'd been warned was coming, he found himself more frightened than he'd been in Vietnam.

"Why can't we go to a tunnel alcove?" he'd asked Colin when he heard the train whistle at the approach to the tunnel.

"Because you need to learn this, Bob," Colin replied.

"We're quite safe here as long as you hold on to the rail real tight." The main danger with fast trains, he'd added, was that you could be caught in the slipstream and pulled under.

The train seemed to be bearing straight down on them.

"Are you sure we're in the right place?" Johnson yelled.

"Just hold on tight!"

The train thundered towards them. Just when he was certain they were going to be annihilated, Johnson saw that it was on a path that took it beside, not over, them. The power of the slipstream was incredible, like an evil force that longed to drag them under. Johnson hung on to the safety rail and prayed. He hadn't prayed in a long time.

"Still like working here?" Colin grinned after the train had passed.

Johnson answered yes. But from then on he listened even harder for unscheduled trains that might use the inner-city circle during their shift. They averaged about two alarms of this kind a month.

On the night he found the amulet, the gang had just survived another unscheduled train. Walking back to the spot they'd hastily abandoned, Johnson caught sight of something glinting on the tracks. He dropped behind and picked it up. It was a man's antique bracelet, made perhaps of pewter. A beautiful piece of work.

Johnson decided to regard it as an amulet. The word *amulet* came up a lot in the fantasy novels he devoured in his off-time. It sounded more mysterious than *bracelet,* and had connotations of power. He shoved the bracelet deep down in the pocket of his overalls. He didn't want it handled by anyone else. It was his.

He kept his treasure hidden through that shift and took it home with him that morning. Usually he'd have breakfast at some greasy spoon, propped in a graffitied booth with the latest sword-and-sorcery magazine he'd bought from the sleepy newsagent in Central Station's main concourse. This morning was different. He went straight home. He wanted to examine his find in peace, and under a good light.

He arrived home shortly after sunrise. He checked the house. Empty. Laurel was out somewhere as usual, catting around. For some years now Johnson had tiptoed around the frail eggshell that was his marriage, taking manual jobs away from home whenever he could get them. Marry in haste, repent at leisure, he thought. Whoever wrote those words knew what they were talking about.

Sometimes, when Johnson looked at his wife, he was surprised to discover that she was still beautiful. But her pale blonde beauty had a brittle quality. She was TV beautiful. He'd married her for her beauty, on the rebound from Star's dark good looks. Now here he was. With his new night job their lives hardly overlapped at all.

Good.

With Laurel out, Johnson felt it was safe to take out his treasure. He switched on the electric stove, tossed a slab of butter into a frying pan, added a T-bone steak, a handful of mushrooms and a sliced onion and sat down to examine the bracelet.

His find was made of some kind of silver. Strange were the hieroglyphs etched into it, unlike anything he'd seen before. They were more like . . . runes. He considered for a moment. Didn't Tolkien's *The Hobbit* have runes on the endpapers?

Johnson rummaged about in the bookcase where the rarely used books were stacked on the bottom shelf. Half the books were romance novels (Laurel's); half were fantasy (his). By the time he'd found *The Hobbit,* his meal was cooked. He forked the steak, onion rings and mushrooms on to a plate, made a cup of instant coffee and sat down with the book, a biro and a notepad. He had a hard time at first. Tolkien never gave the alphabet for runes, only some writing in runes on the front endpapers and its translation at one point in the text.

By the time Johnson had finished his meal he had a working alphabet. With this he set to deciphering the runes on the bracelet. The translation, when he'd finished, read:

To those whose work is still undone,
Wish on the rays of the rising sun.
With this gift you will win through,
Though the fiends of Hell oppose you.

Wish on the rays of the rising sun, what kind of advice was that? Still, Johnson put the amulet back into the pocket of his overalls. Next morning, as he stood on the steps after his shift underground, he noticed the sun was about to rise above the old Grace Bros building across the road from Central Station. Remembering the verse etched on the amulet, he wished hard on the first rays that appeared, but nothing happened. Travelling home later in the bus, he felt like a first-class fool.

From then on, though, he wouldn't go to work without the amulet. He wore it on his left forearm under his long-sleeved overalls. So it didn't do anything, so what? It made him feel special, like the hero in a Robert E Howard novel. It was a little touch of fantasy in a world that was too real. Something to bring him luck in that strange, forsaken underground.

Perhaps the accident happened because the gang was almost out of the tunnel. Colin and Johnson, working ahead, found themselves with no alcoves to retreat to except the ones they'd already passed—and that meant running back, towards the train.

Johnson panicked when he heard the train whistling behind him. He ran out of the tunnel, away from the train and on to the clear tracks. Then he realised that he couldn't climb the face of the sheer cutting to the west, and he wouldn't survive the drop down the steep embankment to the east.

He dithered. Dimly through his panic he could hear Colin shouting, "Back here, Bob. *Back here!*"

By now the train was shrieking like a demon out of hell as it bore down on him. Johnson could hear the screech of metal on metal as the driver applied the brakes. At the last moment Colin came out of nowhere, pushed him into the safety hole he hadn't seen in his panic and tumbled in behind him. Colin knew every safety hole and every alcove. He'd worked the inner-city circle for years.

Johnson huddled there as the lone engine went rushing by. It had been a close call. When the panic subsided and he climbed out, he was horrified to find himself looking at two broken bodies lying on the track ten metres in front of him.

One body was Colin's.

Oh God, Johnson thought. Colin had gone into the hole behind him. He mustn't have had time to get securely in before the train reached them, and the slipstream had pulled him out. The other body was a mystery. It lay, face down, too terribly damaged for Johnson to want to inspect it closely. The train had not stopped. With slipstream accidents, engine drivers rarely knew they had happened until later.

A strange mist began to envelope the scene. The signals at the side of the track disappeared. Johnson's ears were ringing. He felt numb. The rest of the gang had been able to take refuge in the tunnel alcoves. Now they came running. Johnson knew he should wait for the police to arrive. They would want a statement. He knew he should report somewhere for counselling. All he wanted to do was go home.

He drifted away.

Central Station's clock read 5.01 a.m. as Johnson made his way unnoticed through the main concourse and out into the dawn light. It was almost sunrise, no clouds in the sky. He leaned his back against one of the rough sandstone pillars that formed the colonnade at the entrance to Central and tried to push the sight of Colin's body from his mind. A wave of grief swept over him. He closed his eyes as it hit him. Everyone he cared for seemed to disappear or die. Everything he touched turned to rubble.

The sun began to rise over the top of the Grace Bros building opposite; Johnson could feel the light on his closed eyelids. Unthinking, he put up his left hand to shield his eyes from the glare. He was wishing at the time, wishing with all his heart that things had been different. That his kid brother Will hadn't died in Vietnam and that Star still loved him. This world was full of shit. You worked like a dog all your life, then you died. Why couldn't he have been born in a more adventurous time, full of broadswords and magic and glamorous women?

The light hit the amulet, exposed as he lifted his hand against the sunlight. He felt a blinding flash and a sense of impact, as if he had fallen from a great height but had landed upon his feet, unhurt.

Johnson found himself standing on a parapet, his back pressed hard against a rough sandstone wall. The sun was just rising over the ancient city below him, touching with gold the towers and minarets that spread out towards the walls encircling the city. As he watched the alleys below him began to spring into life. In one quarter a bazaar was opening. Merchants led donkeys. Barefoot girls, brightly dressed, carried earthenware pots upon their heads. In the distance he saw the great bronze doors to the city swing open to admit a string of camels, heavily laden, their riders swaying wearily in the saddle.

Johnson pushed open the heavy curtains that draped the window to the parapet and looked inside. Richly woven tapestries hung on the stone walls. Ornate carpets covered most of the marble floor. In a curtained alcove he could see a bed strewn with silks and furs.

In the centre of the room knelt a young woman with

long dark hair held back from her face by a circlet of gold. She looked a lot like Star when he'd first met her twenty years before. She wore golden breastplates and a jewelled girdle, from which hung a long skirt of some filmy material.

She was holding a ten-inch knife to her breast.

"Forgive me, Great Ones," she cried, "for what I am about to do." She positioned the knife against her chest and began to lean on to it.

When Johnson saw she meant business and wasn't rehearsing for a play, he leapt into the room, wrested the knife from the strange woman's grasp and tossed it away.

She jumped to her feet and rounded on him. "What do you here in the chamber of Queen L' Étoile? Have you been sent by the gods to help me?"

Johnson decided to answer yes to this question until he could figure out what was going on. It was like being in a movie, he thought, only he hadn't read the script. He led the young woman to a sofa strewn with cushions.

"What is your name, stranger?" she asked. "From whence have you come?"

"I live in Annandale," he answered. "My name's Bob Johnson." Keep it short, he thought.

"Johnson of Annandale." The young queen considered this. "I have not heard of you. But that matters not if you have come to help me." She rose and, approaching a carved ebony table, poured wine from a carafe into two matching goblets. "It seems the gods have answered my prayers. We will drink to them."

Johnson took the goblet from the young queen's hand and downed the wine in a single gulp. He studied her. On her feet were small silk slippers, encrusted with pearls. On her arms were many bracelets that clinked when she poured the wine. Legs to die for gleamed through the see-through material of her skirt. Well, he thought to himself, he'd wished for glamour.

"P'raps we could have coffee sometime," he murmured.

"You wish coffee, Johnson—you prefer coffee to wine?" The young woman strode to a nearby wall and gave three tugs on a long velvet rope that hung beside a tapestry.

Within minutes a young man appeared, clad in sandals, a broad leather belt and a loincloth. A scimitar hung at his side. He carried a copper tray that held a carafe of coffee and a number of matching cups.

"This is Bildethius," the woman said, "and I am L'Étoile, queen of Parthenia."

The servant bowed as he set down the tray. If he was surprised to see Johnson in his overalls and work boots in the royal chambers, he gave no sign. For a second Johnson was reminded of his dead brother Will, but the likeness was only fleeting. L'Étoile dismissed the servant and poured the coffee herself. All traces of her former distress seemed to have left her.

"Listen, warrior. Tomorrow at dawn I am to be forcibly wed to Yogoroth, the sorcerer who lives in yonder tower." She pointed through the window to a stone tower standing two hundred metres away. The tower rose up from a walled garden whose bushes bore strange black flowers that nodded in the early morning breeze.

Johnson sipped the hot coffee. Now there was a sorcerer to contend with. Well, he had asked for magic. He tried to remember what else he'd wished for. He had a feeling it might have included broadswords.

L'Étoile continued. "My father, Aeides the Wise, died one moon ago. I am his only child, come but lately to the throne. But with nameless rites and many promises, Yogoroth has won the army to his will, and the common people are powerless against him. He plans to marry me and seize the kingdom, for once the marriage is consummated," she shivered, "he will become the rightful king of Parthenia. But I will die before I allow myself to fall into the hands of such a monster."

The same mist he had seen on the tracks after the accident hung for a moment in the room. Johnson rubbed at his eyes to clear it.

"The palace guard?" he asked.

"They are only fifty. I would be sending them to their deaths if I told them to oppose Yogoroth on the morrow. Now let us discuss your plan to rescue me."

But Johnson had no plan. He guessed it was in the script he didn't have.

"No plan! But you are a great warrior from the outlands."

Bob Johnson raked his hand through his hair. Things were bloody confusing. As he raised his hand the amulet on his left arm came into view, glinting dully.

At the sight of the talisman the queen gave a shriek and leapt from the sofa.

"The magic amulet of Zagar! So that is how you came here. With this, you will be able to slay Yogoroth and give me back my kingdom."

Johnson did not answer her. He felt cold. Shock, he told himself, from the accident. The icy, drop-off chemicals of delayed shock were creeping through his veins.

"I will reward you well, of course," L'Étoile said, misunderstanding his grim silence. "Come now, if you do not have a plan, I do."

"Your pardon, my queen." It was the young slave who'd brought the coffee, standing respectfully in the doorway. "A messenger from Yogoroth is here. He would speak with you."

L'Étoile rose to her feet. "Hide the amulet!" she hissed to Johnson.

The messenger was a tall lean man in his thirties. He wore black robes and simple leather sandals. His head was shaved in the manner of acolytes.

"My queen," he bowed deeply. "The great Yogoroth has sent me to ask if there is anything you require for tomorrow's nuptials—silks from the far countries, perhaps; gems from Hydrathistan . . . He commands you—"

"He *commands* me?" L'Étoile drew herself up to her full height. "Get out, you dog. Tell Yogoroth I will see him on the morrow. Go!"

The acolyte backed out, leaving L'Étoile and Johnson alone.

"I don't suppose you've got any beer?" he said.

As L'Étoile summoned the manservant again she said, "Let me tell you my plan."

It was a simple plan, which suited Bob Johnson, who'd always believed that simple plans were best. There was a secret passage, the young queen explained, that would take them from her apartments to the door of the wizard's underground lair. Tomorrow, with the aid of the amulet, they would slay him as the sun rose, and she and the kingdom would be grateful to Johnson for ever.

"If he is underground," Johnson objected, "how will we use the amulet to kill him as the sun's rising?"

"His laboratory is built into a hill. But on the eastern side the land has fallen away to present an insurmountable cliff. The wizard, some whisper, likes to use the power of the moon to enhance his dark spells."

"Show me this secret way," Johnson ordered.

L'Étoile lifted one of the heavy tapestries and pulled on a small metal ring set into the rock. Part of the wall slid back with a grating sound to reveal the beginnings of a staircase, cut into the stone.

"This staircase goes down for ninety steps," L'Étoile told him. "Then there is a corridor three hundred paces long. At the end of that is a stout oak door that leads to the wizard's spell room. It is barred on this side."

Johnson was mystified. "Why build a secret passageway from the royal apartments to a wizard's incantation room?"

L'Étoile withdrew from the top of the secret staircase and worked the mechanism that closed the door.

"Once the reigning king had a great favourite. He loved her so much, 'tis said, that he built that tower for her with its hidden door. But you must be hungry, warrior, after your great journey. Let us eat." She pulled on the velvet cord she used to summon her servants and resumed her place among the cushions on the sofa.

Johnson's eyes took in the queen's slender form as she settled herself once more upon the crimson velvet. He wondered just how far being a great warrior from the outlands might get you in Parthenia.

"And after lunch?"

"After lunch," L'Étoile answered as servants, led by

Bildethius, came bearing great salvers of bread and fruit and a joint of meat, which they set out on the ebony table, "I am sure we can find something to while away the hours until four o'clock tomorrow morning."

Johnson smiled as he settled himself among the cushions. This was definitely a Conan world.

With a clashing of tiny gears, the queen's water clock chimed four hours past midnight. Johnson woke and felt about on the bed.

The young queen was gone.

He rose from the rumpled bed and strode through L'Étoile's apartments. The sitting room showed signs of a struggle. Near the fireplace a small ivory table had been overturned. One of the queen's slippers lay by itself on the carpet beside an upturned candle sconce.

Johnson cursed his capacity for the beer of every realm. He pulled on the velvet rope he'd seen L'Étoile use the day before to summon her servants. Bildethius appeared so quickly he surmised the youth must have been sleeping outside the door.

"Where's the queen?" Johnson shouted, naked, clad only in the long string of pearls the young queen had hung about his neck during their lovemaking.

"She is gone, my lord?"

"Search the palace!" Johnson shouted. "I fear the queen has been taken by Yogoroth before the appointed time."

Soon the palace echoed to the hue and cry of servants searching for their sovereign. Johnson pulled on his overalls and tool belt, poured a jug of water over his head to clear it and went out on to the parapet.

The wizard's tower gleamed in the moonlight. Johnson fished a packet of cigarettes and a lighter from a pocket in his overalls. As he stood smoking he caught sight of a strong steel hook lodged securely under the balustrade's rounded top. From it hung a thick rope. The rope went down over the wall and disappeared among the bushes of the palace garden, where now the lights of searchers' torches showed through the trees. Johnson swore as he pulled up the rope.

Bildethius reappeared. He saw the rope in Johnson's hands. "It is true then. That fiend has taken our queen!"

"Leave me, Bildethius," said Johnson, "I need to think. But continue your search of the palace gardens."

The servant backed away. Johnson strode to the secret door the queen had shown him. Catching up the queen's ceremonial knife, he stuck it into his belt and, holding aloft a flaming torch pulled from a wall cresset, he stepped inside.

The stone steps went steeply down. Johnson could not make out more than a few metres in front of him, but he trusted L'Étoile's description and counted as he went. Just as she'd said, the steps ceased at the ninetieth, and an arched passageway lay before him.

Johnson held one hand out in front of his face as he traversed the corridor. He was expecting to run into spiders' webs, but the passageway was strangely clear of them, and its floor looked to have been swept in recent times. He frowned: the queen had said the corridor was known only to the royal family, and she was the last surviving member of hers.

Johnson couldn't see the imperious young queen wielding a broom. He put the question out of his mind and went on counting his steps. At the halfway mark of one-hundred-and-fifty he began to hallucinate. Was that soot on the walls? It couldn't be.

Johnson was pulled out of these thoughts by the stealthy tread of a person on the steps behind him. He rounded the next corner and an alcove revealed itself on his left, large enough for a man to stand in. He extinguished the torch and pressed himself against the alcove's stone wall, muscles tensed to leap upon the would-be assailant when he was past.

Whoever it was showed no light. Quietly the footsteps came on, with a surety in that pitch blackness that made Johnson's flesh creep. How could this person be so sure of his footing in this unknown place?

When the assailant was one pace past, Johnson leapt from the alcove and knocked the unknown on the head with the butt of the extinguished torch. Then he pulled the queen's knife from his belt and threw himself upon the fallen man.

"My lord, my lord!" cried a familiar voice. " 'Tis I, Bildethius!"

Johnson fumbled in the pocket of his overalls for the lighter. The small flame showed him Bildethius's face. He got to his feet and relit the torch.

"You know about the secret tunnel?"

Bildethius smiled through his pain. "All the personal servants of royalty know about the passageway, my lord," he said. "But Queen L'Étoile, it pleased her to think it was a secret, so I kept it that way. People of royal blood do not stop to wonder why the floors are swept." He rose to his feet. "Let me come with you. The wizard is strong, and two are better than one. See? I have brought you this." He picked up the broadsword that had fallen some distance away when Johnson ambushed him. "Take it, sire," he said, "for I know little of swordplay. It belonged to King Aeides. Also, I have this." From under his belt he produced a small packet containing some kind of powder.

Johnson hefted the torch to see better. "What is it?"

"The dust from the black lotus that grows in the wizard's garden. 'Tis rumoured it gives protection from the Lost Ones of the Pit." He pushed the small packet back under his belt. "And now make haste, lord, for dawn will soon be upon us."

Johnson led on. He tested the weight of the sword Bildethius had given him. A king's sword, no less. At length they came to a stout oak door bound in brass.

"Notice, my lord, the strong bar that secures the door on this side." Bildethius pointed. A great log had been cut in halves lengthways, and one of its halves dropped into iron slots set into the stone on either side of the door. "When our late King Aeides saw how Yogoroth was declining into loathsome practices and foul debauches, he had this replace the original lock that held the door."

"Okay, okay." Johnson was edgy now that he was close to discovering L'Étoile's fate. "Here's the plan: you grab the queen, I'll deal with the wizard. Get back here with her and bar the door. Wait for me in her apartments."

"But what of you, lord?"

"Either I'll kill Yogoroth or he'll kill me. Either way my worries will be over."

The half-log bar lifted easily in the hands of two men. The door creaked open with a sound that made their hearts lurch. Beyond the opened door hung a tapestry, through which they could see into the wizard's den.

The room was hung with curtains of black velvet. On three walls candles burned in cast-iron sconces. The floor consisted of a mosaic, sombre but beautiful. Along one wall ran a bench covered in laboratory equipment. Potions in glass containers stood on the shelves that lined the wall behind the bench. Where the east wall should have been was a gigantic archway. Beyond that was open space, through which Johnson could see the sky.

"You took your time, Johnson of Annandale," a smooth voice said.

The wizard reclined on a sofa, drinking wine from a crystal goblet. He wore a robe of gold silk and a matching cloak of gold velvet. His hair was long and flecked with grey. Johnson found it hard to estimate his age.

"We are lost, my lord," Bildethius muttered.

L'Étoile was sprawled on an altar, her clothes slashed. Her wrists and ankles had been tied with rawhide to chains running to iron rings set in the sides of the altar. A myriad scratches covered her breasts and stomach. Otherwise she appeared unharmed.

"What kept you, Johnson?" the wizard asked. "For hours we have waited for you—haven't we, my dear?" He walked over to the queen and ran his long fingernails across her breasts. She shrank at his touch.

"What do you want with her?"

"She is my pathway—and a very pleasant one, at that—to the throne of Parthenia. Or is that it, stranger—would *you* be king?" Bildethius emerged from behind the tapestry. "Ah, I see you have brought Aeides' faithful pup with you."

The young servant seemed frozen to the spot. "How did you know we were coming, dread lord?"

Yogoroth pointed to a small table, its legs constructed of bones. On its copper surface stood a large ball of clear quartz.

"You thought it was a myth, didn't you, Johnson—wizards and their crystal balls? When my acolyte told me the queen was entertaining a strange warrior in her apartments, I dusted it off, and lo!"

The wizard struck the ball lightly with the staff he held in one hand. The surface of the ball grew cloudy, then L'Étoile's apartment appeared. Johnson could see clearly the queen's fallen silk slipper, the overturned table, the fallen candle sconce. And beyond, the queen's bed.

"Such things I have beheld these past hours before my servants spirited her away. Have you not done with her yet, Johnson of Annandale? I had hoped sometimes that you would leave something over for me and for my pet."

"You could've had me killed while I slept."

The wizard gave a short, sharp laugh. "That would not have been nearly so amusing. Imagine, Johnson: for years I waited for that fool Aeides to die. For years I lusted after his daughter, who never cast an eye on me except in loathing. Locked up in my tower reading parchments all day, consigning screaming peasant girls to death at the full moon, do you really think that's much of a life—well, do you?"

Johnson took his chance and leapt towards the altar. Using the dead king's broadsword, he began to slash at the rawhide bonds that held L'Étoile. He had freed one of her feet when a ray of light from the sorcerer's staff knocked him to the floor.

"Flee while you can, Johnson," the wizard laughed. "Go back from whence you came. The girl is mine."

Johnson's head rang. He fingered the amulet hidden under the sleeve of his overalls, but a glance through the open archway showed him only pre-dawn light. Somehow he must survive until the sun rose.

Yogoroth walked over to a small brazier that burned on the laboratory bench. From an open bowl he took a spoonful of black powder and threw its contents on to the brazier's fire. Unnoticed, Bildethius began edging towards the altar on which the queen lay struggling. He reached it and began hacking at the remaining thongs that held her.

As Johnson dragged himself to his feet the sorcerer spoke. "You don't understand, do you, Johnson? You think you're in love. But I am not so blind to reality. I am going to marry this vain queen and become the new king of Parthenia."

"Never!" L'Étoile screamed. "There is nothing you can devise that will persuade me!"

Yogoroth smiled. Dense black smoke had begun to issue from the brazier. The smoke rose in coils towards the ceiling, forming a column ten feet high that hung in the room. The wizard prodded the column with his staff and muttered an incantation. The smoke began to solidify. Gradually it took the shape of a huge man covered in scales. His head was shaped like a snake's, his forked tongue flicked in and out, tasting the air. He stood on two legs. A long tail hung down behind him.

L'Étoile gave one cry, "The Snake Man of Dagon!" and fainted away.

"That is no good," Yogoroth said. He seized a jug of water from the bench, glided across to the altar and dashed the water into the queen's face. "We want her awake, don't we, Johnson? When he is finished with her, she will come gladly into my arms, will gladly do whatever I bid, knowing this fiend is mine to command. Mind you leave her undamaged," he told the demon. "I intend to breed her with him," he said to Johnson. "Their issue would be pretty, would it not?"

Johnson sprang towards the wizard with sword extended. Yogoroth gestured. A second bolt of light shot from his staff, and the sword flew from Johnson's grasp. Still Johnson came on. Like a running back on a football field, he tackled the wizard. They fell to the floor together, rolling and grappling on the mosaic.

The huge snake man was advancing on the altar, intent on the queen, who'd regained consciousness when the water hit her. When the monster was barely a metre away, Bildethius sprang from his hiding place behind the altar and struck him a blow with the scimitar that would have decapitated a man.

The snake man was undamaged. He batted Bildethius out of the way, raking the side of his head with talons that drew blood. Bildethius regrouped and rushed to the other side of the altar. He managed to sever the last of the young queen's bonds, but now the snake man was upon her. He shoved her back, fighting and screaming, on to the altar.

With trembling hands Bildethius produced the black lotus powder from the packet under his belt and blew it into the monster's face.

The snake man gave a horrible cry and reeled back from

the altar. The queen leapt free and ran for the door to the corridor. Before Bildethius's horrified eyes the demon began to dissolve. Great globs of grey mucus and silver scales fell on to the mosaic.

"The corridor, Bildethius!" Johnson yelled, still struggling with the wizard.

Yogoroth released Johnson and reached for his staff. It lay some distance away on the floor. Seeing his intention, Johnson leapt for the staff and seized it, but he had no idea how to use it.

"My lord, my lord!" L'Étoile cried.

Yogoroth had regained his feet and was hurrying across the chamber, intent on reaching the door to the corridor before Bildethius and the queen. Johnson hurled the staff across the room like a javelin. It struck the wizard squarely between the shoulder blades. He fell to the floor, gasping for air. Bildethius and the queen disappeared behind the tapestry that hid the door to the secret tunnel.

"Bar the door!" Johnson shouted.

The wizard dragged himself to his feet and stumbled to the doorway. As he ripped aside the tapestry the door clanged to. There came the dull thud of the log bar landing in place on the other side.

The wizard hurled himself against the door, but it was as Bildethius had said. It would take a battering ram to bring it down. He whirled on Johnson.

"Fool! Your interference merely postpones my triumph. I command the army and they dare not disobey me." He reached towards a velvet rope, intending to summon men to knock down the door.

Johnson sprang across the room. Yogoroth must not be

allowed to pull that cord. L'Étoile needed time, if only to die in peace. But she would wait to know the outcome of his struggle before doing away with herself; Johnson felt sure of that.

The velvet cord with which the wizard had hoped to summon help had caught on one of the candle sconces. As he fumbled to untangle it Johnson closed with him.

Yogoroth managed to pull the ceremonial knife from his belt. He slashed at Johnson as Johnson hung grimly on to him. The blade sliced through Johnson's overalls and across his stomach. It was only a flesh wound but it bled.

Yogoroth shouted, "I have you, dog!"

He rushed in to deliver the *coup de grâce*, but Johnson was essentially unharmed. He leapt back, tossing Yogoroth's cloak over his head as he closed on Johnson for the kill.

Yogoroth sprang away, cursing, wrenching the cloak from his head. Johnson's eyes swept towards the eastern part of the room, open to the sky. Strong pre-dawn light illuminated the east. How much longer before he could enlist the aid of the amulet?

They circled, knives in hands, Johnson holding the queen's blade, the wizard his ceremonial knife. As they passed by the bench that held the laboratory equipment Yogoroth snatched up a dagger that lay among the pots and jars and hurled it at Johnson with deadly accuracy. Johnson was passing a carved wooden screen the wizard used to curtain off his laboratory area when not in use. The dagger went cleanly through his shoulder and lodged itself in the screen. If he couldn't wrench himself free, the wizard would soon get past his guard and land a telling blow.

The wizard dipped his ceremonial knife into a dish of

green powder that stood on the end of the bench.

"One touch of this, my bravo, and you will be as useful as a dead lion. Ah, but you will have your uses when you awake!"

With a shock Johnson realised that Yogoroth planned to take him alive. It seemed the knife had only to break his skin, and the chemical on it would render him unconscious, probably for hours.

The wizard came on at a run. It was almost sunrise. Desperately, Johnson abandoned his attempts to get free and steeled himself to parry the wizard's strokes. Yogoroth closed. With his right hand Johnson managed to seize the wizard's knife arm and hold it away from him. He held his left arm aloft, exposing the amulet.

The sun rose. Its first slanting rays hit the amulet.

Johnson found himself struggling with the wizard on the railway tracks near the entrance to a tunnel. As he fought to avoid the knife that Yogoroth still wielded, he could hear the rumble of a train advancing through the tunnel behind them. From somewhere, he could hear Colin's voice.

"Back here, Bob. *Back here!*"

Johnson and the wizard stood grappling on the tracks. Johnson wanted only to get away from the train that bore down on them shrieking. Live now, worry about the wizard later. The rails shook, the brakes screeched, the train whistled one long, desperate sound of warning.

The wizard released Johnson at the sound of the train whistle. He spun around to see what demon Johnson had summoned to save himself. Johnson wrenched free and leapt towards the safety hole in which Colin stood shouting. He had one glimpse of the wizard's gold robes billowing in the train's headlights, then the train was upon him.

"Christ, mate," Colin said when the train had passed, "why'd you leave it so late!"

Johnson climbed out of the safety hole and walked to the spot where Yogoroth had gone under the train. Nothing. He walked the tracks for thirty metres in either direction but he could see no sign of the wizard. A thin piece of gold silk fluttered on the tracks at the entrance to the tunnel. He picked it up.

"People are always losing things," Colin observed, coming up to him and fingering the fabric. "They blow down into the tunnels from the platforms. It's expensive. Do you want it for your wife?"

Tears came to Johnson's eyes. "You're all right."

"I was always all right," Colin replied. "It was you we had to worry about." He slapped Johnson on the shoulder.

Johnson turned and began to run back along the tracks towards Central Station. Somewhere L'Étoile was waiting. But how long would she wait before doing away with herself?

He leapt up on to Central Station's main platform and ran up the silent escalators. The clock read 5.05 a.m. as he rushed into the main concourse, avoiding ambulance officers running the other way carrying stretchers.

Panting, he leant his back against the sandstone pillar where his adventure had first begun. Soon, he knew, the sun would rise above the top of the building opposite. Doubts wrenched him this way and that. What if the amulet didn't work this time? Even if it did, should he go?

As Johnson stood, irresolute, a taxi pulled up outside Central Station's main entrance. His wife Laurel emerged from it, shrieking, "Where is he? I must see him."

Johnson made up his mind.

A crowd began to gather. At 5.07 a.m. the ambulance men returned carrying two bodies on stretchers. Laurel had to be forcibly restrained. At one point in her frenzy she broke loose and rushed straight towards Johnson as he stood against the sandstone pillar, watching.

She did not see him.

Johnson pulled the talisman from his pocket. He held the object aloft.

The sun rose over the top of the Grace Bros building. Its first rays hit the amulet. Johnson saw again the white light, experienced again the odd sense of impact.

Then he was gone.

13

Star Sees the Light

2006

Yesterday I fell in love with a field of giant sunflowers. I saw them when I was watching daytime TV with an ice pack on my face. They were growing somewhere in Russia, I think.

I couldn't get over those sunflowers. I stopped eating, my mouth fell open. I just sat there and stared. I remembered a poem by D H Lawrence, "Poverty," I think it was called, where he talks about some tree "pluming forth and being splendid". That's what those sunflowers were doing, with their yellow heads as big as dinner plates.

I slapped on a lot of make up, jammed a sun hat on my head and bought two packets of giant sunflower seeds uptown. If I plant them now, they'll be ready at Christmas. That'd be nice: if they were standing there, pluming forth and being splendid when my mother came for Christmas-New Year. That'd show her that everything is all right.

That'd show her how well I'm coping.

There's just one problem. The only patch of ground that's sunny enough has a lot of large basalt boulders in it, and I can't shift them.

I plan it carefully, my campaign to get Wayne to clear that piece of ground. I get my hair done and wear the blue dress I know he likes. I make veal with cream and marsala and I get in a lot of alcohol. After dinner, when I ask him if he'll dig up the area on the corner of the drive and remove the rocks, he says, "Sure. No worries."

I plant the seeds in a polystryrene box on the front verandah. They're up in five days. Over the Sunday roast dinner I tell him—carefully—that the seedlings will need planting out at the end of next week. Will he have the rocks moved by then?

"Sure," Wayne says. Smiling. Pouring gravy over his potatoes. "No worries."

A week goes by. There's no sign of the promised flower bed.

"Look," I say carefully; I don't want to provoke him. "I'm going to get Barry to come over and move those rocks for the sunflower bed. You're much too busy, and those plants need to go out now."

"Don't nag, Stella. I told you I'd move 'em, didn't I? I'll do it tomorrow."

Tomorrow turns into Saturday. Over lunch he says to me, "I'm going down to Ballina this arvo and I won't be back 'til ten o'clock. Keep dinner for me, will you?"

"What about the sunflowers?" I ask.

But he's out the door and gone.

Another week passes. The sunflowers are thirty centimetres high.

"I'm going to give these sunflowers to your mother," I say. "Somebody might as well get some pleasure out of them. She can put them in that flower bed along the front fence."

That gets him. "What if I plant them now?"

I shake my head. It's high noon. The sun is cruel in the sky.

Two hours later, though, a sudden set of clouds comes over. I tell him he can plant the seedlings now, if he likes, because it looks as if it's going to rain.

We go downstairs, Wayne carrying the polystyrene box of overgrown sunflowers. He can't find a shovel, and I'm so upset I can't remember where I put the hand trowel.

He picks up a paint scraper. "Can't these damn plants just go in among the gardens we already have?"

"It doesn't matter where they go," I say. "They won't grow now, they're too advanced."

"You're being a bit pessimistic, aren't you?" Wayne says, digging little holes all over the garden and even in the lawn with the paint scraper.

The sun comes out from behind the clouds just as he's finished. Straight away, the plants begin to wilt in the fierce sunlight.

"Aren't you gonna water 'em?" He smiles at me like someone who's just won a point in a tennis match.

Love Nil.

I water the plants although I know it's pointless. Then I go upstairs to do the washing up. As I'm standing at the sink, rinsing the dishes under the hot water before putting them into the dishwasher, the tears come. I try to stop them but I can't; I'm too far gone.

He sees me when he comes back upstairs. "What's up with you?"

I can't say anything. I just stand there, rinsing dishes, crying without a sound.

He comes up behind me and puts his arms around me. But I can see the whole game plan now and I turn stony. I discovered a long time ago that he can't hit me until I take him back. I stay stony. It's different from the apathy. There's a hardness in it. I don't care any more what happens. Whether he hits me, whether he kills me.

I don't care.

Wayne's confused. You can see it worrying him. I don't care about that either. I'm safe in a space I've never found since the day I married him.

He starts to make phone calls; he's calling in his debts. I don't know why, but that's okay with me because I don't care.

One day I hear him say, "You found it? Great. Fix you up later, mate."

He organises a babysitter and takes me out to dinner at the best restaurant in the shire. It's a long time since he's taken me anywhere, but it doesn't mean anything to me now.

I don't care.

When the wine's flowing like there's no tomorrow, he hands me a small gift-wrapped box.

"Well, unwrap it!"

I unwrap it slowly, trying not to tear the expensive paper. Inside is a necklace of small, exquisitely crafted sunflowers made of 24 carat gold. It's just large enough to fit around my throat.

"Put it on," he says.

I do, fumbling a bit with the clasp.

"There," he says. "They'll last longer."

Strange how something small can sometimes set you free. Next day I start packing, and I'm gone within the week.

"I don't get it," Wayne says every second weekend when he comes round see the youngest, who's still living at home. "They were only flowers. It wasn't like they were worth anything. They were just flowers."

14

Yesterday, Today and Tomorrow

2013

He hears them, you understand. And yet he doesn't hear them. There's no point in listening, he thinks; it's the same thing every time.

"Good morning, Mr Lawson, and how are we today?"

Answering these girls is pointless, he's decided. They aren't really asking a question. It's a greeting, something to say. People have to say something to each other when they're strangers.

He drinks his cup of tea in silence and gives thanks for small mercies. He thinks it tastes like stewed paper, but at least it comes. It's something he can rely on.

The sun's out today, so the residents get to sit in the garden between morning tea and lunchtime. The trees are very beautiful at this time of year and, although he can't see well, he can tell there are lots of brightly coloured flowers in the garden.

"It makes the place look so cheerful," Matron says. But Lawson knows you can't pick them. When he had his own place, he always grew flowers as well as vegetables, always liked to have cut flowers in the house.

The painters are here again. Seems to Lawson they're always painting this building.

" 'Scuse us," they say as they carry their ladders past him.

He doesn't answer them.

"Wonder what he's thinking," says the dark haired one, the one who reminds Lawson of his grandson Rocky.

"Prob'ly nothing at all," the other one says. Coarser. Fairer. "You know what they're like at that age."

Let me tell you, BoyO, thinks Lawson, you won't get to my age at the rate you're going with all that weight. If you do, you'll be looney. Like Iris, who wanders the hallways, crying "Don't Daddy, don't". Or old Colonel Henry, who commanded an entire regiment in the Second World War, and now sits, drooling.

Mrs Everton thinks she's in the hotel her husband used to take her to when they were courting.

"It's a beautiful place, Mr Lawson," she says to him. "The gardener does a wonderful job. I think I'll have my wedding reception here."

"You do that, Mrs Everton," he always says. Why burst her bubble?

Some days, though, Lawson thinks something gets through to her. Those days she looks upset and spends her day staring out the window. When the nurses ask, "Wouldn't you like to watch TV?" she waves them away.

Maisie thinks her children are going to come and take her home. She packs to go home at least twice a week.

Lawson's never seen these children, not in five years. He sits in his chair by the window and watches her, when he's not watching the birds. She perches on the bed, fully dressed. Waiting for them.

When the sandwiches are brought around at five o'clock, and the nurses make her take off her brave little hat with the pansies and swallow a Valium and change into her nightdress, she seems to resign herself.

"They must've been held up," she says to Lawson. "But I'll keep my port packed. That way I'll be ready if they come early tomorrow."

Everyone's mad in the place but me, Lawson thinks.

Friday afternoon. The clock hangs on the wall. The visitors sit, dejected, tired of searching for something to say. In the Activities Room, the Friday afternoon community singing starts up.

> *"By the light, [By the light, By the light],*
> *Of the silvery moon, [Of the silvery moon],*
> *I want to spoon, [I want to spoon],*
> *To my honey I'll croon love's tune . . ."*

"Why don't you come? It'll do you good," the little nurse's aide named Cinnamon says to him. Surely that can't be her real name, he thinks. For a second he's tempted to go, just to see her smile. But he prefers to go to North Beach.

North Beach, in the summer of 1933. He was ten. Sap rising.

Every Sunday the launch *Kelvin* makes two trips from

Mullumbimby to Brunswick Heads and back. It moors at the boatshed in the river, just round from the Heads.

Lawson and his brothers race over the gangplank and tear along the path through the bush to the beach. Behind them, their father carries the baby. His mother and his Aunt Ellie carry the picnic baskets.

Ah, the ocean! It's like magic after being on the dairy farm all week.

They stand on the sand near the bamboo lifesavers' tower and tear off the clothes they've got on over their bathing costumes. Lawson's always the last one in. He doesn't care. He never goes far out, just splashes about near the shore and, when he's tired of that, he walks along the beach, collecting seashells in his sun hat.

His mother and his aunt sit under a she oak, wearing large hats tied with scarves, and never ever go in the water. He stays away from them. They'll only want him to help them put out the food for the picnic.

"Boys should learn these things, too, Charlie," his unmarried aunt says at least twice a week. He doesn't listen. Everyone knows preparing food is woman's work.

When the whistle sounds, they have fifteen minutes to gather their things and get back to the boat. He hates having to leave; he wants to stay there for the rest of his life. He dreams of ways he could make this happen. But he always ends up catching the boat back with his family.

"Honey moon, [Honey moon, Honey moon],
Keep a-shining in June, [Shin-ing in June] . . ."

Sometimes, though, especially lately, he thinks he might

rearrange that memory. Why does he have to go back and work on the dairy farm? He wants to paint; he's good at it. In his new improved memory, he builds a cabin behind the dunes out of bits of old timber washed up on the beach, swims naked in the river every morning, falls asleep to the sound of the sea.

He buys groceries at Brunswick Heads, wading across the river at low tide. And he paints. The walls of the cabin are covered with his paintings. When he's eighteen, a handsome art dealer down from Brisbane on a holiday falls in love with him and takes him back to the city with him. He becomes famous and holds art exhibitions. What a glamorous life they lead!

But he can never hold on to that fantasy. Always it blurs and starts to fragment. What about when it's dark—what about money? Reason comes crashing in like the sea in a cyclone, and he has to catch the boat back, after all.

Some things you just can't change, he thinks.

> *"Your silv'ry beams*
> *Will bring love's dreams,*
> *We'll be cuddlin' soon,*
> *By the silvery moon.*
> *The . . . sil-v'ry . . . moon . . ."*

The sandwiches arrive, so Lawson knows it's five o'clock. He doesn't mind. Tonight, after lights out, he's decided to go to Mr and Mrs Reading's house at North Beach with his wife. They looked after the Readings' house at North Beach for their honeymoon, he and Angela, in 1943. Two days, they had. That was all the leave he could get.

A wooden cottage with lattice on the verandahs, and no power. At night, they lit hurricane lamps, geckos fell from the rafters into their soup and the scent of the eucalypts mingled with the smell of the sea. There were spiders in the outhouse, and sometimes snakes. But Angela wasn't afraid of anything. She could ride and shoot and swim. She used to go so far out on her bodyboard that Lawson would be frightened, just watching her.

In 1977 he asked his daughter Thea to take him back to North Beach. They drove to the site in her American car. There was nothing there. Only the bush and the new rock walls, and the sea breaking.

The cottage, the boatshed, the lifesavers' tower—all gone. As if they'd never existed.

He'd searched the spot where the cottage had been, but all he found was a small piece of lattice.

Time rolls over them like the ocean. The painters arrive again. Lawson sits in his wheelchair under a jacaranda blazing with colour. That's all they are to him now; just patches of colour. A breeze shakes the branches. He puts out his hand and, like a miracle, one flower lands in his palm.

Most people believe jacarandas have no scent. Ah, but they do, he thinks: a fine light fragrance that makes his heart thud strangely in his chest.

He holds the flower tightly and closes his eyes as the painters go by, carrying their ladders. It's such a beautiful morning that he goes to North Beach with Angela. They walk up the beach to the New Brighton store and send postcards to all their friends. ***Wish You Were Here.*** Of course they don't, but sending the postcards is fun.

In the evening after dinner, they stand on the dunes and try to spot ships passing out at sea. Hard to do because they're all blacked out. Angela stands on the dunes with the sea wind blowing her long white nightdress against her legs and, against every inclination he has, he loves her.

There: they see the dark shape of a troopship going north on the horizon. Someone moves a blackout curtain in one of the landside cabins. For a moment, light spills from the porthole.

He and Angela try to imagine what it must be like to go on a ship to Europe, the way well-off people did before the war. They joke: someday they'll go to Ireland, to County Cork, and look up their parents' relatives.

But the sun is so strong today Lawson can't stay with Angela and the troopships. Instead he finds himself at North Beach in 1933. The boat's just docked and he's running as fast as he can, trying to beat his brothers to that first glimpse of the sea.

Later, he lies down under a she oak. Let the boat leave without him this time. When he wakes, there's a harvest moon rising slowly over the ocean. It makes a silver path on the water. For an instant, he's so excited his heart

stops.

But it starts again, and he walks into the water.

He follows the silver pathway. The sea is warm. Angela's on a bodyboard way out where the waves are breaking. He can't hear her for the sound of the sea, but he knows what she's saying.

"Come on, Charlie, you've got to do it sometime!"

He wades into the ocean towards her. He can't swim and

yet he's not afraid. He knows that when he reaches her, she'll put out her hand and help him up on to the board. And then they'll go to Ireland, just like they planned.

He wades along the path made by the moonlight. He keeps his eyes on Angela and walks into the sea.

Back on shore, the painters are talking.

"I sure wish I knew what he's thinking," the dark haired one's saying.

"You blind?" the other one says. His voice comes faintly now to Lawson as he and Angela sail away on the silvery sea. "He's not thinking anything, he's

just . . .

asleep . . ."

15
Pilgrimage

2014

It didn't seem at all like the place she remembered. THAT HOUSE, FLOATING THERE IN HER DREAMS.

It was raining as they made their way along the dirt track to the end of the ridge where the house had stood. Three days of rain had made the track treacherous. The light drizzle soaked Azure's cheap jacket, supposed to be a raincoat. She didn't know where she was until she saw the mango tree.

Twenty-seven years . . .

A LITTLE RED PEDAL CAR. A TRICYCLE. A SIAMESE CAT IN A YOUNG MANGO TREE. That young tree was huge now, larger than all the other trees in that dark grove.

She had known the house was demolished, but no one had warned her how the bush had taken back the clearing. Only one post where the back porch had been remained to show there had ever been a building there.

"Was this yours, Azure?" her newest man asked, kicking at a lawnmower rusting among the weeds.

She wasn't sure. Maybe it was, maybe it wasn't. Though she'd had a mower once. She could remember O'Neill pushing it in the evenings, complaining at the rate the grass grew, while the air smelled sharply of eucalyptus.

Twenty-seven years.

She searched the undergrowth for the garden she'd lain awake at night, planning, the garden he'd dug for her in the harsh shale of the hilltop. There might be something left.

Something.

She walked about, looking with fresh eyes at this strange place, no longer her Dreamtime.

Then the climbing rosebush caught her eye, its roses red as blood. She'd planted it six weeks before she had been forced to leave the property—O'Neill long gone to Brisbane, cursing snakes and the rural lifestyle, all on fire for his new life in the karate world. She'd just begun to train the rosebush up a wire to adorn the walkway from the kitchen to the side steps.

THE KITCHEN'S SCRUBBED PINE TABLE WITH THE HERB POTS. THE BATTERY OPERATED RADIO, NO POWER.

She'd had no car after O'Neill left, no phone and no electricity. "How did you do it?" people said to her later. But she had prayed never to leave the spot.

LET ME DIE HERE.

Now the rosebush struggled among the lantana, the groundsel and the Jimson weed. But it was there.

THERE. SHE WAS ON HER KNEES IN THE SUN, TRAINING THE FIRST FRAIL RUNNERS UP THE WIRE.

There was nothing else.

Not a pot. Not a candlestick. NOT A CHILD (LONG GONE,

TOO) RUNNING UP THE BRIGHT SLOPE WITH A SCREW-DRIVER IN HIS HAND. "I FELL OVER, MUMMA!"

Gone, that fierce cleared land, that view of the sea, that sense of isolation and clarity.

Gone, the carpet snake, the loneliness, the sounds in the night that had caused her to buy a gun.

She hadn't known, as she grubbed in the ground, afraid now of white men, that down the hill on the land behind the dunes was an old Aboriginal initiation site.

Men's business.

But they had been good to her, the lone woman with the young boy.

She'd known she was somewhere sacred. Every evening, as she lit the hurricane lamps and pulled the heavy curtains in the old farmhouse, she had prayed them away, the two of them, into the night.

WE WILL NOT DISTURB ANYTHING.

They had exhausted their time there.

"How do you feel?" he asked as they turned to go.

Azure pulled a rose from the besieged climber. "I don't know. It's all so different." She couldn't explain that feeling sad was not the same as being depressed, though she knew how he feared her depressions. And she was hanging out, couldn't wait to lock herself in the bathroom with the gear.

On the way back to the car she became tangled in the barbed wire fence the new owner had erected. She hadn't got caught on it on the way in.

It took him ages to release her. He'd get one piece free and she'd be caught on another.

Stuck there.

Getting into the silver Mercedes, she paused to push the rose into her hair and caught sight of her face in the rear-view mirror. Her long blonde hair was turning grey. She was becoming irrelevant.

On the drive back to the highway she fought off panic. Was memory enough? She didn't think so.

What was it O'Neill had said during their last break up?

"Perhaps in some other lifetime."

On the day he'd made this pronouncement, Azure had thought he meant reincarnation. But maybe not. They had their DNA in that data bank, put there when O'Neill had been obsessed with his psychiatrist. Maybe he'd meant that.

Either way, it was small comfort.

16
Another Lifetime

2137

It was my job to watch, not to intervene. That was the problem. Bodyguards were rare on Earth in 2137, but Thurston must've figured the experiment of a lifetime needed protection—or maybe he just wanted a witness in case things went wrong later. I don't know.

I watched on the monitor as he ushered her into the office. She was fragile and beautiful, very much the dancer. Her thick, rich hair fell down to her waist. It was the colour of ripe maize. I sat in the cubicle, watching, listening.

Thurston was speaking with an undertone of excitement in his voice. "What you're suggesting is incredibly dangerous, and the procedure would be irreversible. *If* I were inclined to do it, which I'm not." He leaned back in the antique wooden chair he insisted on using and looked at her over the top of his half-moon spectacles. He wouldn't wear lenses. "You mightn't survive the operation."

The afternoon sunlight shone in through the stained glass windows of the old one's study. I could see the dancer analysing the patterns they made on the floor—or was she analysing her chances?

Thurston pulled a pipe from his pocket and began to stuff it with the coarsely ground *tobacco* leaves that he bought on the black market and kept in a worn round tin in the second drawer of his desk. An ancient habit, *nicotine,* so out of date and fashion this alone would have revealed his great age. The dancer waited in silence. Soon the smoke reached her from across the desk, and I think she adjusted her sensors.

"What about your wings?" Thurston asked suddenly, as if he wished to catch her off guard. But it seemed she had prepared herself for this.

"They'd have to go," she said simply.

Thurston shook his head. He was a small man with light bones, blue eyes and thick, silver-grey hair. His clothes were old-fashioned. He was considered eccentric. But he was the Director of Genetic Engineering and had been for more than twenty years.

"Come now, Azuria," he said.

So that was her name. Strange, it rang a bell with me, but a quick search of my data bases did not reveal the reason. Had the DNA used for me known the DNA used for her—was such a transmission even possible? Another thing I didn't know.

"What made you decide to come to me?" Thurston was saying.

Azuria smoothed a fold of her gold robe. All flyers wore robes; there was a particular colour for each profession.

Winged dancers always wore gold.

"I know you can do it." Her voice was soft and clear, graceful as her robe. "I think I've always known."

The old guy busied himself with some papers—another one of his weird habits: papers. I noticed his fine, blue-veined hands tremble slightly and I read in him an undercurrent of something I couldn't define.

The dancer was easy. She came straight to the point, and I wondered if she was malfunctioning. She was asking him to make her human. No wonder he wanted a bodyguard with top security clearance. No wonder he'd made me the offer he had.

I spoke into my headpiece. *May I remind you, sir, that under Federation law the penalty for performing what she is proposing is death.*

Thurston shifted another paper to acknowledge my message. He let Azuria think her proposal had surprised him. Yet he had known her request in advance. Why else had he asked for my services?

"You're the best winged dancer in the five districts." The tone of his voice invited her to confide in him. "Now why would you want to give that up?"

She lied. How do I know she lied? It's my business. I'm an INFJ, an old term but still valid. My intuition levels are way above the norm and my judgments are ninety-five point three per cent correct. That's the best you can buy, which is why old Thurston picked me, no doubt.

I inhaled two crushed crystals of off-world Blue Monday and watched her lie. Whatever she hoped to gain by persuading Thurston, she wanted very badly. The light passed from the stained glass windows, and still they talked.

She strung words together like strands of pearls.

And in the end, the old man nodded his head.

"She's lying," I told him after she'd gone.

The blue eyes took on a steely glint. "Your people can't lie, Michael. It's not in their genetic programming."

I sat in a wrap-around and watched her coming out of the anaesthetic. Thurston had a reputation for genius. Now I saw why.

Azuria looked . . . human. It was more than the absence of wings. Something indefinable—the glow—was gone from her.

We were in an old stone cottage in the country in the Western District. In the back garden were trees, some of which were in bloom, and high in the late afternoon sky my people were wheeling, amusing themselves as they always did at the end of the day.

Thurston followed Azuria's gaze to the open window. He waved the medical droids away and ran a hand through his silver hair, betraying a rare agitation.

"Azuria," he said, "this is Michael. He's a security expert. He'll be with you for the duration of your project."

She looked frightened.

"My dear," the old fox said, "you must see the need for total security."

I watched her eyes wander again to the open window.

"Michael will live with you and work with you," Thurston went on. "He'll be on hand at all times. To protect your interests, as it were." He smiled thinly. "We'll pass him off as your assistant."

I got to my feet and smiled at her. "Love your hair."

Azuria put a hand to her head. "My hair! What have you done to my hair?"

It was now black, darker even than my own, and cropped short in the current fashion of female science execs I'd glimpsed in the corridors of power.

The professor shot me a look that'd melt metal. "All right, all right," he said to her. "So I changed your hair, and your face a little. You were very famous." He began to walk about the room, searching for his aerokeys, which he'd left on the shelf above the antique fireplace.

"I've arranged for you to become research assistant to Dr William Elliott, as you requested. His research facilities are three miles from here. You'll commence as soon as you're fully recovered." He'd found the keys. Now he paused in the doorway. "I leave you in good hands. Michael here will brief you on your new identity; there's a file in the computer. Relax. Michael here has all the instructions."

He neglected to tell her that my instructions included a weekly report on her For His Eyes Only, and that what I couldn't get by being there I was to get out of her in other ways—if necessary, by surveillance.

"One other thing," he said to her. "I've built in the reproductive system. As you requested. You'll have normal, female hormonal fluctuations, but remember this—are you listening?"

Her eyes had strayed to the window again. Night had fallen while he was speaking. High in the sky, wearing lightbands around their heads, my people looked like characters out of an ancient fairy tale.

Thurston went on. "You must never become pregnant.

Bear that in mind, Azuria, and take the appropriate precautions."

He was gone. I went over to the wall unit and punched out a drink. I wondered why he'd given her a reproductive system if using it was going to kill her. Sexual differentiation we'd always had: some of us ended up as personal companions. But reproductive systems?

No. We were not a species.

Azuria had fallen back into sleep. I pressed off the bedside lamp and sat in the dark, watching her. A medical droid hovered in, examined her smoothly, expertly.

"She will not wake again tonight, master."

"Stay with her." I dropped my robe and pulled on a bodysuit. Then I snapped a lightband around my forehead and joined my people out in the dark moonless sky.

She was now, according to the files, Dr Azuria Eastman, computer big wheel, and I was her assistant with a security clearance from the president himself. As a result of The Thirty-Year Fear, my people were banned from working in the top levels of any of the scientific disciplines, and wings were built into our DNA so that the ban could be easily enforced. So my clearance was necessary.

Az passed for human without a hitch. The stiffness of her gait we put down to a recent aero accident, and as time went by it disappeared altogether.

Dr William Elliott was Director of Psychology for the Western District. He was thirty-five, tall and gangling, with deep-set dark eyes and an IQ in the human population's top one per cent. He'd been hunched over a computer since the age of three. Now he verged on being a sensana, with few social skills and no ability to make conversation that was not directly related to facts.

Az took absurd pains getting ready for work each morning. She agonised over her clothing. Elliott didn't know she was on the planet. Every morning he turned his head from the monitor he was working at, flashed her a smile that never reached his eyes, and that was it.

In the area of computers, humans had it hard compared with flyers. They could not, as flyers could, interface with the main computer, thus saving what might amount to months, if the data was complicated. The psychology department was underfunded and overworked. Elliott was exhausted all the time. I figured Az's chances of getting his attention were close to zero.

Which was fine with me. Sensanas are bad news.

Two moons went by. Then Azuria began to work late. At first I stayed back with her, but computechnology is not for me. Once I was certain Elliott wasn't staying back, too, I went home at the usual hour like everyone else, ensconcing myself in front of the VR machine with a steady supply of Blue Monday, the complete video collection of Azuria's past triumphs, and an ache I couldn't quite explain.

So I missed the cues.

The first time Az stayed back she couldn't get out of bed the next morning. She retched intermittently for seventy-two hours, then she was her normal self again. When we returned to work, Elliott made a great fuss of her. He even hugged her. Then he dumped reams of computer printout on to her desk, telling her to take as much time off as she liked afterwards but to get him results the way she'd done before, and once again he said, “You’re brilliant!”

I’d never seen him so animated. But then, he was talking about work.

Az did this two more times; she was in bed for a week after each occasion. Thurston, hearing of Elliott’s sudden breakthrough, came boiling on to the videophone.

“You fool!” he shouted. Behind him in the VF screen I could see the same stained glass patterns that had been reflected on the floor all those moons ago. “You fool, don’t you realise what she’s doing? She’s interfacing with the main computer, her new system can’t stand it. She’s no use to me dead! Stop her, Michael, see to it.”

I relayed the professor’s message to Azuria in softer hues.

“It’s all right,” she said. “I’m sorry if I got you into trouble, Michael, but I got what I wanted.”

Then she told me: just before I’d arrived home from work that day, Elliott had called in to the cottage to see her, something he had never done before. He was high on the breakthrough her figures had given him.

He asked her out.

In the past, Az told me, *out* for her had always meant that her company would be entertaining somewhere that night, dancing and flying in one of the five huge theatres with their high ceilings and strangely decorated surrounds.

Standing in the wings, listening to the overture, she said she’d run a last-minute comb through her long gold hair. She always danced with it loose. It was for her a prop as important as the costume itself. Even the *maître de danse,* an eminent authority on arcane dancing, gave up and allowed her to perform with her hair unbound. It paid off, he knew. The public loved it. Besides, it wasn't good for the company to have such a disturbance as Az could create when she didn't get her way.

"Ah, Azuria 27," she said the *maître* had said to her one night as they were waiting in the wings for their cue to go on, "there's a flaw in you somewhere. Watch out for it. Some day it will be your undoing."

She'd laughed when she told me this, but I knew what the dance master had meant. There was something strange about Azuria. Something different.

Out had another connotation. It meant the flying my people did every evening just on dusk. Again, Az said, she'd worn her hair loose. She liked the feeling of the wind whipping through it.

Most flyers liked to fly high, just below the domestic airlanes and well above the billboards. Az liked to fly low. She had, she told me, an obsession about gardens. Old-fashioned ones with rosebushes were her favourites. She'd come down neatly between one bush and another, snatch a rose, push off with the foot she was balancing on and be gone, all in a matter of seconds. Later, she said, she'd take the rose back to her compartment and put it in water, if the flight home hadn't torn off all its petals.

One evening a wind came up unexpectedly. After she'd snatched the flower she wanted and went to push off into the deepening sky, she found that her hair was caught on a tall rosebush. As she stood there, struggling to free her hair and becoming more entangled in the process, Elliott came out from the back of his house and cut her loose with a pair of scissors.

He couldn't have been as worn out as he was when I met him, for he made a lasting impression on Az. She found out who he was, then she went to Thurston. That was the beginning of it all, of the strange, unnatural life she was now leading.

Thurston was very pleased with this report. "She told you all that? Good work, Michael, good work."

I accompanied Az the night she went out with Elliott. I went with the second-in-charge of his department, a woman called Helena, who fancied me. She'd had her face done over the previous week to look like the Mona Lisa.

I wasn't interested.

The home of the Director General of Science was set on a hill with a commanding view of the countryside. It was built in the old style, of stone and glass, and furnished with every luxury a human could attain. In her gown of clinging gold mesh, sheath-like and slender, the new Azuria was a shock to both of us in the ornate, wall-sized mirrors, her black hair looking to me like some kind of ill omen.

The head droid led us to a table for four. We helped ourselves from a selection of drinks on a tray held by an impeccably clad android that hovered unobtrusively nearby.

"You should enjoy the entertainment this evening," Elliott said to us as we were finishing the elaborate dinner.

I doubted it. Humans weren't much good at entertaining themselves any more. In just two generations their sport and performing arts had fallen into decay. Who could compete with a flyer programmed especially for the purpose? Still, there were pockets of resistance.

The Director General, Elliott continued, possessed a stage almost as large as the Great Hall's. He indicated the red velvet curtain that covered one end of the gigantic dining room. The Director General had engaged a company of dancers for the night.

"Flyers?" I asked cautiously.

"They're human," Elliott replied.

Just then the lights dimmed, the orchestra struck up and the dancers came on. Elliott indicated the soloist he wanted us to see: a small girl, very dainty, with neat, clean footwork and good elevation. For a human.

She had long, ash-blonde hair, which she wore free in the style Az had made famous.

I got through the show by drinking everything the android had on its tray so that it had to excuse itself and go for more, and planning a paper on sensitive analytic personalities—sensanas. How did they do it? I wondered. How did they know just where to put the knife?

After the show the girl Elliott had indicated came to our table and sat down. She was a personal friend, he said as he introduced us, "going back," he said, "to childhood."

The girl smiled at us. Her name was Cassie. "We went to school together," she said, still watching Elliott. "Our mothers are old friends."

The Mona Lisa made much of her. But I could see that the kind of personal history that Cassie had just expounded, and with which Az could never compete, distressed her.

"Azuria's a computer genius," Elliott went on, oblivious of the angst on our side of the table. "She's the one responsible for my breakthrough happening as fast as it did."

Cassie smiled at Az with her honest brown eyes. She hitched the loose wrap that covered her costume back on to her shoulders. "I'd love to do something academic but it isn't possible. There's no time when you're a dancer."

"Tell me about it," Az said in an undertone.

"Well," Elliott said to Cassie, "in your case it's worth it. After all, how many *great* dancers are there?"

I pulled Azuria gently to her feet.

"William," I said, "I'm taking her home." Away from this barbarous house and your weird way of thinking. "She's still very fragile." I'd completely forgotten about the Mona Lisa.

"I'll take her," Elliott said. "You go home with Helena."

To The Director of Genetic Engineering:

Transcript of tape: Dr Azuria Eastman to Michael 64, 10 June 2137, Veracité dosage 40 mgs, administered to the subject in coffee.

Dr Eastman speaking:

At first, I didn't recognise the house, approaching it from the front as we did, but when we entered the library and I looked out through the large windows, I recognised the garden. Bathed in moonlight, the rosebushes stood as I remembered them. Elliott has the best rose garden in the five districts.

He brought me a glass of something yellow, punched himself a drink of a different colour, and we went out on to the terrace. He said he had something to tell me.

I leaned against a trellis covered in lavender flowers and was silent. Just to be in that garden was unnerving, and now there was the new development of the girl Cassie, something I hadn't allowed for in my calculations.

"Do you remember what the department was like when you first arrived?" Elliott asked me. "It was a madhouse. Every evening when I got home, I used to punch myself a drink and sit in the dark in my study and watch the winged beings; just watch them. You know how they like to fly in the evenings just on dusk?"

I nodded. The garden lay very still and quiet under the moon. The scent of roses was all around us.

Elliott continued. "There was one winged being who used to come every evening and steal my roses," he laughed. "I used to watch for her. She was the most beautiful thing I'd ever seen, so graceful . . ."

I had begun to tremble uncontrollably. He didn't notice.

"One evening," Elliott went on, "it was windy. She got her hair caught on one of the taller bushes. I raced out and cut her loose with a scissors." He punched the balcony with his fist. "I should've used the opportunity to meet her, to find out who she was! But she was panicking, getting ripped up by the thorns; I was afraid for her wings. So I cut her free, and the instant I did, like that"—he snapped his fingers—"she was gone."

By now I could barely stand. Still, Elliott didn't notice. He took me by the hand and led me back into the house saying, "I want to show you something. You're the only person, apart from Cassie, who's ever seen this. I showed it to her the night I broke off our engagement."

He went to his desk, lifted a piece of fabric from a drawer and unwrapped it.

"Look," he said. "I went out next morning and got it off the rosebush. You know I never saw her again."

There, under the lamplight, nestled in a piece of black velvet, lay a long coil of my golden hair. My erstwhile golden hair. I fell to my knees and began to sob. I couldn't seem to get enough air.

Elliott knelt down beside me. "I'm sorry," he said. "I didn't mean to upset you." He was stroking my hair and he moved on to my shoulders. "Don't cry . . . don't cry . . ."

Of course we ended up in bed.

REPORT ENDS HERE.
Michael 64

Elliott will never know how lucky he was that the government outlawed Ethyl Alcohol way back in 2100. Sometimes, when they were together all night, I fantasised about getting hold of some on the black market, then going round to his house and beating the bulk out of him. But Thurston would've pulled me off the case.

I'd already had one run-in with Thurston when I'd asked him for the hidden agenda on this case, and he'd refused me. I toyed with the idea of giving up the undercover assignment, but jobs with remuneration like that don't come along very often, and I had some expensive habits. Besides, there was Azuria to consider. I felt I owed her something. Don't ask me why.

Two more moons passed, then Thurston called me into his office again: Azuria wanted to see him urgently. Once more I watched her secretly on the monitor, once more she came to the point straight away.

She wanted him to change her back to what she'd been when she first came to him.

Thurston shook his head. "I warned you at the start that was impossible." Then he asked her what had happened to bring her to this point.

She told him she was pregnant. "And," she added, with a playfulness that reminded me of her former self, "sir, I am not yet dead."

Thurston gestured with a fragile, blue-veined hand, as if to wave away this facetiousness. "You must have a termination right away."

Az shook her head, and that desperately dark hair fell on to her forehead like a curse.

"My dear," Thurston said carefully; he was into the *nicotine,* which seemed to help him focus. "It isn't conceiving that'll kill you. Obviously. It's the process." He was picking his words the way someone might select pebbles on a beach.

"Have you heard of Doyle's Failsafe, or The Thirty-Year Fear?" He took the pipe from his mouth. "Doyle was our previous director. I worked for him when I was in my twenties. I was exiled during The Fear. I was in favour of giving flyers reproductive systems and letting evolution take its course. Turned out, no one could abide the idea that humans were merely a link in the evolutionary chain.

"That, in a nutshell, *was* The Fear. By the time I returned, Doyle's Failsafe was in place, a neat little genetic modification no one's been able to break. After that, if someone modified a flyer so that she could conceive, the foetus would be sterile. More: the development of the foetus would cause the flyer's death."

Az thought for a while. "Would I live long enough to produce the child—would it live?"

"I might achieve that much; but no more. I can't break through what Doyle's done. He was a brilliant man. Totally dedicated to human supremacy."

"Is he still alive?" she asked too quickly.

Thurston shook his head. "He was many years older than I." He reached for the VF. "I'll order a laboratory with top security and perform the termination myself tomorrow."

Az jumped to her feet. "At least give me time to consider!"

"Sit down, Azuria," Thurston said. "I shan't coerce you."

May I remind you, sir, that under Federation law the penalty for aiding and abetting the destruction of a flyer is death.

Thurston inclined his head. "A timely reminder. The fact of the matter is, we are all outside the law."

We returned to our work in the Western District. I was a lot rougher on Az than Thurston had been, threatening to expose both her and him to the Federation. But, of course, I couldn't. Thurston had made sure I was just as involved as he.

Days dragged by. The only good thing about them was that Elliott was absent; though it galled me to see Az hanging on his return.

When Thurston had heard nothing from her within four days, he came online, looking stern and worried.

She hung her head and simply said, "I cannot."

Thurston sighed. He took me in, hovering unhappily in the background.

"Very well, Azuria," he said. "I'll send you my paper."

"You have written a new paper?" She was pleased for him.

Thurston shook his head. He seemed tired a great deal these days.

"It's not a new paper, it's a very old one. It was suppressed. Read it and then ring me back." He studied her face intently, then he seemed to decide something. "Ring me soon, Azuria."

The screen went blank.

Elliott returned that evening. I had taken the opportunity provided by his absence to plant a number of highly advanced surveillance devices around his house. They were everywhere except the bedroom. I couldn't have borne that.

Az and Elliott made small talk through the meal. She'd evidently decided to hit him with the news after they'd eaten. Elliott appeared preoccupied, and I sensed danger. At length, he pushed his plate away unfinished.

As the droid moved in to remove it he said, "I have a great apology to make to you, Azuria."

I had his dining room on one monitor and a video of Azuria 27 dancing in the Great Hall at the height of her fame on the other.

I waited.

Az didn't speak. She was wearing a black velvet dress with narrow shoulder straps that set off her shoulders and the fine shape of her head.

"I thought you might've heard by now." Elliott spoke from the bar as he dispensed the drinks. "It's all over the

Central District."

Azuria's face assumed a mask of calmness.

"Cassie and I are engaged again," Elliott said in a rush. "We're going to be married. This time it's going to happen."

The dark haired Azuria in the black velvet dress looked very small and vulnerable on one monitor. On the other, Azuria 27 leapt across the stage in a swirl of light and silk and colour.

Elliott came back to the table with the drinks. "Don't go to pieces on me now, Azuria, you were always so much stronger than me. And wiser. I want you to understand: Cassie's different. She's not the being in the garden—and I told her that, of course—but she's the closest thing I'll ever get to it."

Az spoke carefully. "Did you ever search . . . for the flyer in the garden?"

"She died," Elliott said simply. "I saw the records. It's unusual for a flyer to die so young, but it sometimes happens—some flaw in the DNA processing. I went to Professor Thurston myself. I saw the records."

Az drove back to the cottage and crawled into bed with Thurston's paper, which had arrived by special courier that evening. I'd already read the work, which was entitled, *Foetal Cannibalism: a hypothetical study of Projected Terminal Changes in a Gestating Being of Manufactured Origin.*

The type was old with time, and sometimes faded. But the message was clear.

I was on Thurston's doorstep at dawn next morning. He

opened the door wearing a dressing gown and strange footwear.

"When did Elliott come to see you about Azuria 27?" I demanded. "Was it before or after her first visit to you?"

"Calm yourself, Michael." Thurston walked ahead of me into the kitchen. "Perhaps she'll change her mind about the termination."

I had the feeling I was being toyed with, as small animals called cats had once toyed with smaller ones called mice before they killed them.

"And if she doesn't change her mind?"

Thurston had started grinding coffee beans in one of his old electrical machines. He didn't answer.

I picked up a bean and studied it. Coffee beans were grown off-world. They were almost as expensive as Blue Monday.

"Why don't you find a surrogate mother?" I said. "It's Elliott's child. Give it to Cassie. She needn't know, we could drug her."

"All those years of research you did for your Ph. D. on the criminal mind seem to have rubbed off on you, Michael. There's just one problem: what if the foetus is winged?"

"When did Elliott come to see you about Azuria 27?" I asked again. "He says you showed him the records of her death."

Thurston steered me to the front door. "It's not relevant, Michael," he said. "Keep the bean."

The door closed on me.

When Az woke up that same morning, I was ready for her. I

handed her a cup of coffee and began.

"I know you lied to Thurston in that first interview. This is what you were planning all along. Just tell me why."

Az shook her head in a beaten fashion. "I didn't know I couldn't get pregnant. The professor never told me until afterwards."

"But he told you after. I was there."

"I didn't believe him. Couldn't."

"What do you mean, *couldn't?* And whatever gave you this wild idea in the first place? And now you know it'll kill you, why won't you give it up—you won't, will you?"

Az dissolved into tears. "I can't give it up. It's like an obsession, like something hardwired into me!"

"Look," I said. I was now prepared to do whatever was necessary to save her life and keep her with me. "There's a way."

She lifted her face to me, more with curiosity than with hope, fixed me with those clear grey eyes.

"Change your face and hair back to Azuria 27's. And let Cassie be the surrogate mother. The baby will live and you'll get Elliott. That's what you wanted, wasn't it? You made The Change for Elliott, didn't you?"

"The professor said it isn't possible. He said such a thing can't be done."

"He's lying. I know people who can do it."

"Cassie would never agree."

"We drug her."

Azuria was horrified. "WE DO WHAT!?"

"Face facts, Azuria, it's your only chance. You're going to die if you don't do something soon. Think about it."

I found a drug that, administered in the right amount, would produce unconsciousness within fifteen minutes. Too much would kill, but the dosages by weight were well documented. If Az were to ask Cassie to lunch, dose one of Cassie's drinks at the end of the meal, then drive her back to the cottage, I could be waiting with a few of my friends from the old days—I knew a fine *in vitro* gynaecologist and a top plastic surgeon, both of whom could be bought and/or persuaded.

I chose the restaurant with great care. It was set in the 1950s, and situated on the top floor of the highest building in the Central District. It was the only restaurant in the five districts that had a special permit from the government to serve Ethyl Alcohol for the ambience. If Az misjudged the timing of the drug, if Cassie stumbled on the way out . . . well, patrons often did, being unaccustomed to alcohol. And the waiters were human; they could be bribed. If anything went wrong, Azuria was never there.

I had told Az to wait until the last course. With this was always served a very strong, ruby-red wine. This wine would be a perfect cover for the drug, of which only four millilitres were necessary.

"Look!" Cassie exclaimed. "The birds have arrived!"

Birds were a special feature of this restaurant, another part of its 1950s ambience. Each day at a certain time they paraded along the specially constructed parapet outside the glass walls. I had counted on them to provide a diversion.

Az told me later that she dropped the four mls into Cassie's goblet before she, too, turned to look. It was said the early genetic engineers had modelled the wings of flyers on the design of birds' wings. Now birds were almost extinct.

Cassie had been to this restaurant before with Elliott. "See those birds there? They're called doves. Wait until *they* fly!" She leaned across the table and fixed Az with her innocent brown eyes.

"Do you believe in souls?" she asked suddenly. "You know: the old religion that says that when you die there's something inside you, something imperishable that lives on. Do you believe in that? *I* do."

"I don't know," Az said. The idea disturbed her. "Do flyers have souls?"

"No, no, silly. They're manufactured."

The doves took off as Cassie finished speaking. It was a clear and cloudless day. The two birds hung white against the deep blue of the sky. Az felt something wrench in her heart.

"Look!" Cassie cried in a kind of ecstasy. As she turned away from the table for a better view of the two white birds, Az reached out and exchanged Cassie's glass for her own.

"To us!" Cassie exclaimed, turning back to Azuria and picking up the wine glass.

"To us!" Az picked up the goblet containing the drug intended for Cassie, and drained it.

Within fifteen minutes she had driven back to the cottage, where I was waiting in turmoil with everything and everyone ready.

She managed to land her aero, though she hit the antique chimney. We dragged her out of the wreckage, and when I saw that she was unhurt I paid off the surgical teams and sent them away.

Summer ended. Autumn came quickly. Elliott left with

Cassie to take up an associate professorship at the Central University. He never knew about Az's pregnancy.

When Azuria couldn't go to work any more, I quit work too and got in a medical android. In the warmest part of the day it would help her outside. She'd lie on an all-weather sofa and watch the leaves turning from green to gold on the trees in the backyard, while I sat inside with the Monday and watched her.

On dark moonless nights, when she felt up to it, I took her flying with me, wrapped in a thermal cloak. Together we'd soar about the heavens, I in a kind of bliss to have her there, safe in my arms. I was careful not to fly too high. Up in the rarified air, flyers had been known to lose consciousness, blackout and fall to their deaths. It was a great chicken game with young male flyers. Every so often, someone would go too far, and people down below would think they saw a falling star.

Sometimes I'd ask myself why I hadn't intervened. I'd had everything I needed that day to have her terminated and give her back a major part of her original persona. But as Thurston said to me once when I was shooting that vein, what might she have done afterwards? She was obsessed with having the child.

Thurston came every evening. He was failing fast. You could almost see him hanging on. Thurston would outlive her, I knew, and it seemed that was sufficient for his purpose. He had plans, and more support than anyone might have imagined; but I didn't ask questions.

In the evenings he liked to walk in the garden. At first I used to accompany him. Later I preferred to remain indoors with Az. Together we'd sit and watch the old guy walking, stooped, among the roses, his droid hovering nearby.

One night the air was especially chilly, and he came in early, carrying a single red rose, late for the season.

"And so, Azuria," he said, placing the rose in water in a small brass vase on her bedside table. "What do you make of it all, this being human?"

He seemed so jaunty that I said, "The results of the tests have come through?"

Thurston nodded. "Do you know, my dear," he said to Az, "your child isn't sterile? That's why I'm happy tonight." He went over to his battered briefcase and produced a strange, long-necked bottle made of brown glass. "Here, have a glass of stout with me. It'll do you good—the iron, you know."

I glanced a question at him.

"I got it on the black market," the old rogue said. "After all, this is a special occasion. I used to love the stuff, y' know. Never saw any harm in it myself." He levered open the strange bottle's top with a metal object he took from his pocket, and poured three glasses of the brown potion.

Az had to hold her glass in both hands. I made a mental note to get lightweight containers from now on. We drank. Az and I made faces.

"Isn't anyone going to ask why Azuria's child isn't sterile?" Thurston stood before the fire, a slight, bent figure, holding the cut-crystal glass. "I'll give you a clue," he said. "The drug you took, Azuria, the one meant for Cassie, was steroidal."

"Hormone-based," I broke in, remembering the black marketeer's explanation for the exorbitant price.

"A few days either way," Thurston gestured, "and it

wouldn't have made any difference to the development of the foetus. Ah, even in biomechanics there's an element of luck." He drank deeply from his glass, then held it up. "To you, William Doyle! You were a worthy adversary, but I beat you." He topped up my glass and Az's and refilled his own. Then he lifted his glass to her. "To us, my dear! The creators of a new species."

"You need more than one being to create a species," I said, suddenly uneasy. "A species must, by definition, be able to reproduce itself."

Thurston drained the rest of his glass. His eyes blazed with excitement. I'd never seen him like this before. "A thousand winged females, perhaps, Michael. Programmed for maximum genetic variability. And a thousand male humans—it's not hard. With this breakthrough, the progeny won't be sterile. And I think we can avoid this problem," he waved a casual hand at Az, "in the next generation. Of course, that first two thousand, they'd have to fall in love and mate, but that can be programmed too. You can even program a love for roses, y'know."

I choked on the stout.

Az lifted her face to him. "Did you program me to fall in love?"

Thurston smiled at her. "What a question."

An ancient prophet once said, "Let he who is without sin cast the first stone." I went to the window, inhaled the Blue Monday and looked out at the night.

High, high above the bare branches of the treetops, my people were wheeling in slow, lazy spirals against the moon.

END

Publication Acknowledgments

"Busting God" was published in *Blue Crow, Vol. 1, Issue 2, October 2010.*

"Star's Story" was published in *Cutwater Literary Anthology, July 2009* under the title "No Through Road".

"Remains to be Seen" won the *Ulitarra*-Sheaffer Pen short story competition in 1993 and was published in *Ulitarra No. 4, December 1993.*

"David's off his Meds" won the Inaugural Nicholas Shand-Beach Hotel short story competition in 1997, was published in the *Byron Shire Echo, 9 September 1997* under the title "A Happily Married Man".

"So long, Baby" won the 1998 Nicholas Shand-Beach Hotel short story competition, and was published in the *Byron Shire Echo, 22 September 1998,* under the title "The State of Grace".

"Stella by Starlight" was published in the Christmas edition of the *Australian Women's Weekly, December 2008.*

"Star Sees the Light" and "A Dark Place" as one story entitled "The Sunflowers" was published in *Wellspring, Vol. 2, Issue 9, Jan/Feb 1999,* and later in the anthology *From the Circle of Women, Volume 1, January 1999.*

"Transference" was published in *Australasian Penthouse, December 1990.*

"While There's Life" was published in *Below the Belt: Experiences with Prostate Cancer, 2015,* under the title "The Kid".

A condensed version of "Yesterday, Today and Tomorrow" entitled "A Pink Rosebush and a Piece of Lattice" won the Ed Gaskell Award, and was published in *Age Matters*, Lismore City Council, 2002.

"Pilgrimage" was published in *dotlit* (formerly *Imago): the Online Journal of Creative Writing, Vol. 4, Issue 1, August 2003.*

"Roses" was published in *Aurealis, Issue No. 24, September 1999.*

For readers interested in the writing process, the genesis of many of these stories can be found at:
https://goo.gl/w4rGUW

Other books by this author

Fiction. 211 pages. Meet the Katt family. Despite the love in their little cottage, they're finding it hard to make ends meet. When Claude loses his job and the bank won't grant more time to pay the monthly mortgage fee, the Katts are in danger of losing their home. It's up to Claude and Mao and Jacko, the blue rabbit, to discover a way out of the impasse.

A feel-good book for anyone feeling down.

Fiction. 383 pages. Brisbane, 1961. The Pill is not available to unmarried women, pregnancy terminations are illegal and being gay is a criminal offence. Dara Mohoney, a budding artist, has fallen for childhood friend Joe Gordon, who's hoping to make a career in international music. They are desperate for one another, but know that marriage will end their chances for a career. What will they do?

Listed by *Kirkus Reviews* in **100 BEST Indie Books of 2022.**

www.ingramcontent.com/pod-product-compliance
Lightning Source LLC
Chambersburg PA
CBHW031326170626
46807CB00002B/598